NO ORDINARY LOVE

PART 5 OF THE
"LOVE, LIES & LUST" SERIES

MZ. ROBINSON

G STREET Essence

Robinson

Published by:

G Street Chronicles
P.O. Box 1822
Jonesboro, GA 30237-1822
www.gstreetchronicles.com
fans@gstreetchronicles.com

Cover design:
Hot Book Covers, www.hotbookcovers.com

ISBN 13: 978-1-9384425-7-5
ISBN 10: 1938442571
LCCN: 2013931239

Join us on our social networks

Facebook
G Street Chronicles Fan Page
G Street Chronicles CEO Exclusive Readers Group

Follow us on Twitter
@GStreetChronicl

Part 1
The Love, Lies & Lust Series

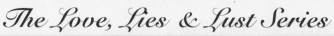

G STREET CHRONICLES
~ PRESENTS ~

WHAT
WE WON'T DO FOR
LOVE

A NOVEL

The Love, Lies & Lust Series Begins...

MZ. ROBINSON

MARRIED TO HIS Lies

A NOVEL

Mz. Robinson

Part 3
The Love, Lies & Lust Series

G STREET CHRONICLES
~ PRESENTS ~

"What would you do for love?"

THE
Lies
WE TELL FOR
Love

A Novel

The *Love, Lies & Lust* Series Continues by Best Selling Author

MZ. ROBINSON

G STREET CHRONICLES
~ P R E S E N T S ~

Love LIES
AND LUST

PART 4 OF *THE LOVE, LIES & LUST SERIES*

MZ. ROBINSON

Acknowledgements

To my Lord and Savior, it's in You that I move and I have my meaning. I thank you for the blessings that you continue to shower upon me and for your grace, mercy, and love. I know without a shadow of doubt that I am nothing without you and I am humbled and grateful that you (and only you) can make Something out of Nothing!

To my mother and father: Mommy you told me to pray, believe, and doubt nothing. Thank you not only for those words but for loving and praying for me. I love you "Pretty Girl". Daddy, you have always told me that I could be anything I wanted to be. I carry those words in my heart daily. I love you and thank you for everything.

To my families: The Caudles, Leslies, Turners, Massey, Walkers, and Rice, I love you ALL! To my Uncle Kenneth aka Bay, thank you for being there time and time again. When we call you come and you come even when we don't. That's love. To my cousin Kenyetta, you are just like your daddy. You have a beautiful spirit that illuminates the room whenever you enter. I love you "Sunshine". To my sister Banita Brooks, we don't talk every day or half as much as I would like but know the love is real.

To Maurice "First" Tonia: Thank you for keeping a smile on my face and always knowing what to say to make me laugh. It's a blessing to have you in my life and every day I thank God for you. ~ Love you ~

To my assistant Shawnda Hamilton aka "Girl Friday": You are one of the hardest working women I know and I'm so grateful for you. Thank you and much love!

To George Sherman Hudson: Whenever I question myself you always remind me of the "gift" I've been given. Thank you for that. It hasn't always been a smooth ride on "the street" but it has definitely been worth it! I am forever grateful. Shawna A.: We may not always know the plan but God always puts the right people in our path. Thank you for your encouraging words and the moments of laughter. They mean a lot to me. I admire your courage and salute your dedication. You are a wonderful example of a woman's actions speaking louder than her words. ~Love and Loyalty Always~

To: Robyn Traylor, Andrea Anderson, Denia Turner, JeaNida Luckie Weatherall, Jewel Horace, Barbara Love, Sheila Jones Weathersby, Keisha Woods, Samantha Pettiway, Lisa Bryant, Timiska Martin Webb, Mary Green, Shanika Dewey Greenleaf, Lisa Dewey Chambliss, Jo'Lynn Dewey Pierre, Jo'Licia Dewey, Brittany Dewey, MarQuita Drayton, The Entire Dewey Family, Althea JustBeing Me, Me'Tova Hollingsworth, Shanta Shaw, Lashunda P. Lee Cato, Trenya Arrington, Susan Vincent, Shan Gradney, LaBrina Jolly, Karena Cowan, Naomi B.

Johnson, Malika Richards, Danielle Churcher, Zakkiyah Karamel Hibbler, Nelly Hester Alejandro, Juanesia Faulks, Taylor AC, Nikki Johnson, Jenelle Challenger, Angela Clark, Tracy Mc Phaul, Pam Thomas, April Streets Palmer, Ayanna Butler, Karyn Gilyard, Nekisha White Bell, Denise Wiliams Cherry, Dee Marcus, Amy Ackerson, Dawn "Cupcake girl" Jay, and Justin Davon Price. "Thank you" is not enough to express my gratitude and my sincere appreciation for all the love and support. I am so honored and humbled! I Love and Thank You All! Special Shout-out to Jacole "Coco" Laryea for your assistance with my "Havoc on a Homewrecker" giveaway, the love you show, and your support. Love and Thank you!

To all my Divas and Kings who take the time to share their lives with me in Books and More with Mz. R: I love you! ~ To everyone on the Love, Lies, and Lust fan page and Mz. Robinson fan page, Thank you!

To the Just Read Book club, The G Street Chronicles CEO Exclusive Readers, Page Turners Book club, Bayou Divas Readers Club, and the United Sisters Book club: Thank you!! To all the other book clubs, stores, and vendors that continue to show me support and love, Thank you! To Kisha Green and the Literary Jewels: Thank you!

To my Editor: Thank you! To Hot Book Covers: Thank you!!

To : Author Katavious Ellis, Authoress Blaque, Fire & Ice, Author V. Brown and every author in the G Street

Family. We are destined for Greatness! Let's Get It! To Chandra GStreet BG Armstead: Thank you for always riding with and being a part of our G Street Family!!

If there is anyone that I forgot, please blame the voices in my head and not my heart!

To every one with a wish and a dream: P.U.S.H.

~Kisses~

Dedication

I dedicate this book to each and every person listed in my acknowledgements. I don't have enough words to express my gratitude for the love and support that I've been shown from each of you. Just know my heart is overflowing with thanks.

~Kisses~

"...With love we must be willing to sacrifice and expose ourselves like an innocent child with disregard to the world or it's scrutiny. We must accept there will be moments of sadness that come in the midst of our joy and understand that any and every thing worth claiming and holding onto is worth struggling and fighting for..."

~Mz. R

Chapter 1

Octavia

I sat with my fingers locked together with Damon's while anxiously awaiting the verdict in the trial of Leon Douglass, aka Gator. I had been waiting for this day to come for well over a year, and now that the moment had arrived, I felt bittersweet relief. Living through the trial and testimony had been hell and had led to the onset of so many unresolved emotions regarding the destruction of a portion of my family.

I know that Gator wasn't responsible for everything that proceeded the day I was snatched outside my car while my daughter looked on. I also know that he had nothing to do with the deaths of my best friend and her husband, but the events had taken place so close together that it was difficult for me to think of one without reliving the other. Maybe in some small way I felt that if I at least got justice for Gator's role in my abduction and his plot to murder Damon, I would have some form of solace when it came to the loss of my loved ones. I cut my eyes to the right, observing the facial expressions of the seven women and five men that comprised the jury, each member looked like they had been through their own personal hell. It was obvious the court sessions had taken an emotional toll on them as well.

The trial, which lasted four days, was emotionally and physically draining on me, but I was positive it was all going to be worth it. Twenty-four hours earlier during the closing arguments, the petite blonde prosecutor described in vivid detail my abduction, and the blood bath that had taken place the final night Gator and his henchmen held me and Lena hostage. I was on the brink of tears as I watched her pace back and forth across the floor of the courtroom, recanting my story with such eloquence and passion, you would have thought that my story was her own. She pleaded with the jury for them to find Gator guilty and make him ultimately pay for his sins against me and other voiceless victims. I was moved by her words; however, Gator, on the other hand, seemed utterly unfazed. During the trial, he sat with a smug look on his face and eyes as cold as the North Pole. Dressed in a dark designer suit with a crimson red silk tie, Gator's demeanor was more like that of a king being toasted by his subjects than a man facing a life sentence in prison. It was clear that Gator was overflowing with confidence that the end of the trial would weigh in his favor.

Why wouldn't he think that? Reality dictated that he

could. In a separate hearing, Gator had been acquitted on several other charges including racketeering and extortion. I, and probably every other adult in the city of Huntsville, Alabama with a functioning brain, knew Gator was guilty as charged; however, he had managed to slip right through the system without so much as a slap on the ass for those charges. The justifications behind the dismissal of the charges ranged from lack of evidence to inconsistent testimonies and even the failure to appear by key witnesses. I knew all the trumped-up reasons for letting him walk were lies. The truth of how he got off on those charges was based solely on the fact that Gator's reputation preceded him wherever he went, and his money seemed to take the "im" out of impossible.

I was hoping for better results in the current proceedings. After all, the DA had strong and accurate witness statements from me and my husband. There was even testimony from my employee Amel, who told of her experiences while being around Gator and his team when she was in a relationship with Beau. I hoped all of those things would help for a different outcome.

Gator's attorney, a chocolate, slim brother who looked like he was fresh out of college, maintained that Gator was an innocent man who had merely gotten caught up in his brother-in-law's emotional tirade. He stood firm on the notion that his client was a family man who only wanted the best for those he loved.

"My client is a man of honor and respect," he said. "A family man who believes in the power of love and whose love knows no limits. My client is the kind of man who practices the principle of honor and exercises loyalty. Ladies and gentleman of the Jury, my client is guilty. But guilty of what? Of choosing to stand by his family? Guilty of being in the wrong place at the wrong time? Guilty of being his brother's keeper? Yes! Those are the only things my client is guilty of."

I listened in disbelief, as he continued giving a speech that was laced with so much bullshit that I felt like I needed to grab a tissue and wipe my ass. I stared at one of the jurors, a young woman with light skin and wide eyes. That heifer had the nerve to wipe tears from her eyes! She was nodding her head like she agreed with each one of the lies that were being told to them. I wanted to run over and knock the breath out of her ass and give her something to really cry about!

I managed to maintain control of my emotions and got through the trial without an emotional outburst, but I couldn't promise the same outcome once the jury gave their guilty verdict. All I could hope was that I wasn't going to hop my pregnant behind out of my seat and shake it like the entire courtroom was making it rain! The jury foreman rose to make the announcement I had been waiting for. I ran my hand across my swollen belly, flinching slightly as the baby growing inside me kicked me again. It was the tenth kick in less than twenty minutes, and if I didn't know any better, I would have sworn he or she was trying to tell me something. I took a deep cleansing breath attempting to calm my nerves.

"Are you okay?" Damon whispered in my ear. I nodded my head yes then closed my eyes. I said a silent prayer thanking God for bringing this part of my journey to an end. I asked Him to continue to bless me and my family as we continued down the road to recovery. I even asked Him to bless Gator's wife—who was the only member of his family present—with understanding and peace.

"Have you reached a verdict?" I heard Judge Gillian ask.

"Yes, your honor we have," I heard the foreman say. Damon's grip on my hand grew tighter. I felt the calming peace of victory as I waited impatiently for the woman to continue.

"On the count of conspiracy to commit murder, We the Jury find the defendant: not guilty. On the count of kidnapping in the first degree: not guilty; unlawful confinement: not guilty; accessory to kidnapping: not guilty." she sighed.

Come again? I opened my eyes darting them in the direction of the woman. She lowered her head then sat down. I looked at Damon assuming I had heard the woman wrong. The expression of shock and disbelief on his face confirmed that I had heard correctly. They found Gator not guilty on every freaking count!

"Are you serious?" I blurted aloud, releasing Damon's hand. I rose from the covered bench staring at the jury. "Have you all lost your minds?" I screamed. "That son of a bitch is guilty, and each and every one of you knows it!" I breathed heavily while pointing at Gator. "How much did he pay you?" I accused as tears began to fall from my eyes.

I felt Damon's hand on my back. I heard his voice in my ear advising me to calm down, but his words were useless; all of my mental reasoning had evaporated. I felt a burning sensation inside of me as my anger overflowed. "You're going to let this sick piece of shit get way?"

Gator turned around looking at me with eyes swimming with what I can only describe as satisfaction.

"Order!" Judge Gillian stated, slamming his gavel.

"You think you've won?" I ranted, glaring at Gator.

He stood slowly then adjusted his tie. He extended his hand to his attorney, and then leaned over and kissed his wife who was sitting on the bench behind him. "Is that all your honor?" He asked.

The judge asked if all twelve members of the jury were in agreement. When they stated they were I excused myself; storming out of the courtroom with my husband following closely behind. There was a swarm of eager news reporters and camera men standing on the courthouse steps asking for my comment as I made my way towards my husband's car.

"I hope he burns in hell," I mumbled.

Damon ordered them to step back as he stepped quickly to my side. I knew that Gator had also made his way out of the courtroom because I could hear a bombardment of questions being asked, like: "How does it feel to be a free man?" "Did things go as you anticipated?" "And what will you do now that this is behind you?"

As I looked back, I glanced up at the steps and locked eyes with Gator. He smiled brightly then winked his eye at me. *Bastard!* I thought.

I climbed into the passenger's side of my husband's Range Rover, still attempting to process what had taken place in the courtroom. I watched as Gator strolled down the remaining steps with a smile on his face; followed by his wife and the media. There was a white-stretch limo with dark tinted windows parked against the curb in front of the spot where Damon and I were waiting for traffic to clear. Gator assisted his wife into the back of the car, and then walked away from the limo headed in our direction. *What the hell?* I thought to myself. He came up to the passenger side window, standing outside the door, staring at me.

"See you soon," he said. He chuckled then adjusted the lapels of his jacket before turning to walk away.

I felt a breeze of air as my husband jumped out from behind the wheel then walked over to confront him. I felt the promise in Gator's words and a fear of what their commitment might bring. I refused to be a victim to him or any of his shitty associates ever again. I reached underneath my seat, retrieving the 45mm Damon had hidden there. I opened the passenger's side door then stepped out. Damon and Gator stood toe to toe engaged in conversation. I tightened my grip on the weight that I carried in my hand while moving in closer.

"It's not over," Gator stated looking at me. "It's

never—" He didn't get the chance to complete his sentence. I aimed and pulled the trigger letting off three rounds in the area of his heart. I watched as blood poured out covering the shinning alligator shoes he was known for wearing, and his body slumped slowly to the ground. A sharp, almost unbearable pain shot through my abdomen causing me to double over. The pain I was experiencing felt like I was being ripped apart internally. My heart began to race a mile a minute as I looked down at the pavement, staring at the small puddle of my own blood that was surrounding my feet.

Chapter 2

Octavia

"Octavia…Octavia…baby wake up…" I heard a familiar voice say. "Octavia…" I opened my eyes slowly then exhaled when I saw my husband's beautiful face. "Baby, are you okay?" Damon asked, stroking my cheek gently with his fingertips. He was kneeling beside the sofa where I lay on my side covered in a light chenille blanket. I stretched my legs out as much as my body would allow before rubbing my eyes. I was lethargic and slightly dazed as I focused on my surroundings and my vision became clearer.

"I'm fine," I finally answered, pulling myself up in an upright position. The additional weight my body carried at its core was an indication that I was still pregnant and the thoughts I had of Gator had been nothing more than a vivid nightmare. "What time is it?"

"A little after one," he said looking at his watch.

"I can't believe I dozed off that long," I yawned. According to the time, I had been sleeping for approximately two hours. When I originally chose to lie down, it was my intent to catch up on some much needed reading while Damon took our daughter Jasmine to my parent's house. However, from the looks of the book lying on the floor, I hadn't made it past the cover. I love the fact that I've been blessed with the gift of carrying another child, and I know that there are many women out there who wished they could have the pleasure and joy that bearing a child can bring; but pregnancy number two was kicking my ass! I was tired all the time, my feet felt and looked like I was wearing floatation devices, and my nose had spread so far across my face that I could have sworn my face was preparing for a jet to land on it.

Don't get me wrong, I know I'm beautiful regardless of all that, and I want nothing more than to bring Damon's and my unborn child in the world healthy and strong; but I'm anxiously counting down the joyous moment when I can have my body back.

"Are you hungry?" Damon asked. The mere mention of food made my stomach rumble.

"Of course," I said, rubbing my stomach. "Do you even have to ask?"

"Nope," he laughed. "That is why I have the grill going as we speak: Chicken, shrimp, and steaks."

"So thoughtful," I said sincerely. I watched as he picked up the slippers I wore earlier and slipped them on my feet; causing me to smile brightly. It was not only the little things he did that made me fall in love with him daily, but also the fact that my husband was nothing short of my super hero; protective, providing, and always there when I needed him.

"You should expect nothing less," Damon said. He stood up straight then extended his hands to me. I slipped my hands inside his warm palms, allowing him to help me up to my feet. The two of us walked hand in hand through our family room to the kitchen.

"What were you dreaming about?" he asked as we reached the French doors leading to our patio. My mental flashback of Gator and the scene that unfolded in the court room sent shivers cascading down my spine.

"About the trial," I admitted.

"What happened?"

"It was crazy," I sighed shaking my head. "They let him off and I went postal." I filled Damon in on the details of the dream as the two of us stepped out onto the patio. I was greeted by the savory aroma of hickory and mesquite fogging the air while the sun shed a light shade from behind the puffy white clouds crowding the sky. As I told my husband about my dream, I intentionally left out the part where I miscarried. The last thing I wanted to do was put additional concern or worry on my husband's shoulders.

"You don't have to worry about Gator now," he said, pulling out one of the chairs surrounding our patio table for me. "That part of our life is over."

Damon was right. Three months after Damon and

I renewed our vows at his parent's home in Georgia, Gator's trial began. After three days of proceedings and only six hours for jury deliberations, Gator was found guilty of both kidnapping and conspiracy to commit murder. The judge later sentenced him to life in prison. The trial was hard on both of us, but we made it through and justice had prevailed. Which is why I couldn't understand why I was *now* having bad dreams about the man.

"What if the dream was some sort of sign or warning?" I asked, shivering from the thought.

"It was just a bad dream," Damon said, kissing me on the top of my head. "Nothing more." I leaned back looking up at him, finding comfort in his dark brown eyes.

"You're right baby," I said shaking the thoughts from my head. "Just a dream."

He leaned down then planted a subtle, but sweet kiss on my lips. "No worries," he said, pulling away then looking at me. "Okay?"

"No worries," I smiled in agreement. "So what were my parents up to?" I asked, changing the subject. Damon chuckled lightly while walking over to the outdoor kitchen. I waited patiently for his response while admiring his physique. If it were possible for any man to get sexier with every passing moment, Damon would be the man to pull it off. From the low-cut waves that now graced his head to the neatly-trimmed hair that surrounded his mouth and his flawless caramel-colored face. Even the casual look of the turquoise colored polo shirt, dark jeans, and *Gucci* sneakers he wore today couldn't down play his sexy. I felt a tingling sensation in between my legs that caused my nipples to swell to the point that they ached. No matter how exhausted my pregnancy had me, the one thing that hadn't changed was the longing I felt for my man.

"When I left they were getting ready to take Jazz to the park," he answered. He stood with his back to me while turning meat on the grill. "However, I think they were handling business when I got there."

"What kind of business?" I asked curiously.

"You know...business," Damon said, turning around to look at me. He raised his eyebrows then smiled. "The kind of business I plan to give you later." He winked his eye then laughed.

"Aw hell," I blurted out, shaking my head. I knew that my parents were human, but a visual of them getting their freak on was not what I needed at the moment. "TMI...TMI!"

"What?" Damon chuckled again. "Just because they're members of the fifty and over crowd does not mean they don't have needs. Hell, wait till we get their age. I'm going to still be beating it up and putting it down!"

"I know they have needs," I giggled. "But I don't want to think about them. And please believe me baby...you can get it!" The two of us shared loving banter until the phone rang interrupting us. "I'll get it," I said easing up from my chair.

"You sure?" Damon asked, watching me.

"Positive." I wobbled towards the kitchen, walking towards the cordless phone sitting on the kitchen island. "I'm coming!" I snapped, slightly annoyed by the blaring sound of the ringing phone.

"Not yet," Damon yelled from outside. "But you will be!"

"Freak!" I yelled back. I picked up the phone then glanced at the caller ID seeing that the call was coming from the Ambiance.

"Hello," I answered.

"Hi Octavia," Tabitha said from the other end.

"Hi Tabitha."

"Sorry to disturb you on a Saturday," she said quickly.

"There's no need to apologize," I said reassuringly. "What can I do for you?"

"Have you talked to Amel?"

"No, why?"

"She hasn't shown up for work." Tabitha informed me.

"What? That's not like her." I said, staring at the clock on the wall. Amel should have been on the clock over an hour ago. Since I made Amel General Manager of the Ambiance, she hadn't been as much as five minutes late. Hearing that she was a no call, no show, instantly had me concerned.

"I know," Tabitha said, sounding equally concerned. "I was hoping you'd heard from her. I tried calling her and I got her voicemail. I left a message, but she hasn't called back."

"Let me try calling her," I said. "Give me a few minutes and I'll call you back." I ended my call with Tabitha and immediately dialed Amel's number. The phone rang several times before going to voicemail.

"Hey Amel, it's Octavia. Call me when you get this message." I carried the phone with me back on the patio where Damon was now pulling some of the chicken he had been preparing off the grill.

"Everything alright?" He asked, turning around to look at me.

"Tabitha called and said Amel didn't show up for work," I advised him. "And she's not answering her phone—" My thoughts and my words were halted by the ringing of the phone. "It's her," I said, checking the caller ID. "Hello."

"Hey Octavia," Amel said. There was something in her voice that confirmed my earlier concerns that something was wrong. Her voice was low and deep and she sounded like she was either congested or had been crying.

"I was worried about you," I said, "Tabitha called me when you didn't show up for work—"

"I am so sorry," she said, cutting me off. "I meant to call her and tell her I wasn't coming in. I think I'm coming down with the flu or something," she said. "My head and stomach are killing me. I was sleep until you called. Octavia I'm so sorry...I'll get dressed now and go in."

No the hell you won't, I thought. The last thing I needed

was for Amel and her germs to show up at the Ambiance and show out by spreading to the rest of my employees! "Don't do that," I said abruptly. "We have enough coverage and besides, if Tabitha needs help, I'll go in. Get some rest and keep me updated."

"Okay," she exhaled. "Thanks so much."

"No problem," I said. "Let me know if you need anything." After I ended my conversation with Amel I called the Ambiance to let Tabitha know Amel wouldn't be in for the day and to let her know to call me if she needed me.

"I got it Octavia," Tabitha said convincingly. "Enjoy your day. Everything will be fine. Trust me."

"Thanks Tab," I said. I was sincerely grateful for all of my employees and the dedication they showed not only to me, but in the service they provided to our patrons. I knew that even if Tabitha needed help she wouldn't admit it. She was bent on proving that she could manage without me and Amel and she had proven before that she could. When I recently selected one of my new hires, a woman by the name of Marilyn, to be General Manager of the Ambiance 2, I had seen in Tabitha's face that she was disappointed, but Marilyn was simply more qualified for the position.

*****

Damon had made my afternoon with the meal he prepared for us, and I was happy and full, at least for the moment, after devouring the grilled chicken, shrimp, and vegetable medley. The two of us had just retired to our home theater to relax and watch a movie when Tabitha called again.

"Hello."

"Octavia, I'm so sorry to interrupt you again—"

"Don't be Tabitha," I said, "its fine. What's up?"

"It's Amel," she exhaled, blowing loudly in the phone. "She came in and—"

"She came in?" I asked shocked. This should have come as no surprise to me. Since Amel's break up with Tarik, she had turned into somewhat of a workaholic. I think it was her way of compensating for the one thing we all need as human beings; companionship.

"Yes," Tabitha answered. "I thought you knew."

"No, I gave her specific instructions to stay at home."

"Well, she's here and she's not doing good," Tabitha explained. "She came in and went straight to the bathroom and started throwing up. She's been in there ever since… I'm worried about her Octavia. I tried to convince her to let Kaitlyn or one of the other girls take her to the ER, but she refused. I didn't know what else to do so I called you."

"I'm on my way," I said quickly. "Thanks for calling."

"No problem," Tabitha exhaled again. "I'll see you when you get here."

"She is so damn stubborn!" I said, shaking my head.

"Amel?" Damon concluded, assisting me up on my feet.

"Yes," I said, looking at him. I had filled him in earlier about my conversation with Amel, and the thought that

I had that she was going to abide by my request for her to stay home.

"She learns from the best," he replied, staring at me with raised eyebrows.

"I know how to take a break," I said.

"I love you baby, but you're addicted to work," Damon said standing. "I'm almost eighty percent sure you're going to give birth in one of your restaurants. I can see it now. You'll pop lil' man out, give him a kiss on the forehead, and get right back to grinding."

"You are crazy," I laughed lightly. "And how do you know we're having a boy? We could be welcoming another little diva into the world." Damon and I had decided not to find out the sex of our baby. I was betting on a girl while he, on the other hand, was convinced our child was a boy.

"I just know," he said, pressing his palm against my belly. I instantly felt the flutter of the baby inside my belly moving.

"We shall see," I smiled. "We shall see."

"That we shall my love," Damon said, "you want me to drive you?"

"I'm good," I said appreciatively. "But thank you."

*****

I stepped inside the Ambiance and was immediately greeted by the sounds of chatter, clacking silverware and soft jazz. The atmosphere was lively, and it was obvious from the way the servers we're weaving and maneuvering from one table to the other that business was going well. I smiled and waved at Kaitlyn; then headed directly towards my office. On my way to the restaurant I called for an update on Amel's condition and Tabitha informed she was no longer sick to her stomach and she was now resting in my office. I was nearing the office door when it opened and Tabitha stepped out, closing the door behind her. She wore dark slacks and a crisp button down white blouse, the traditional uniform I had assigned to my lead hostess.

"Hey," Tabitha smiled as I approached her.

"How is she doing?" I asked, immediately inquiring about Amel.

"Much better," Tabitha advised me. There was obvious relief in her voice and etched in her olive- colored complexion. "She's in there with the doctor now."

"Doctor?"

"Yes, one of the customer's is a physician," she explained. "She was in the ladies room while Amel was in there and she offered her assistance."

"Thank God," I said, sincerely thankful.

"I know," Tabitha sighed shaking her head. "That girl is too stubborn for her own good."

"I agree," I said, nodding my head.

"She had a fit when I told her you were coming, but I didn't know what else to do."

"You did the right thing," I assured her.

"Well, I'll be upstairs in the lounge if you need me," she said, stepping past me.

"Thanks again," I smiled. I knocked on the door then waited until I heard Amel say come in before I entered. Amel sat, reclining on the velvet sofa positioned against the wall, with a folded, wet towel resting on her forehead. She wore a light blue blouse and tan dress pants. Her natural hair was pulled neatly on top of her head in a tucked bun. It was obvious from the slightly off color of her skin, and the faint red surrounding her grey pupils, that Amel wasn't feeling well; but she looked extremely stylish none the less. The doctor was a thick woman with cinnamon-colored skin and short tapered hair. She wore a plain, soft pink eyelet dress and brown wedges. She sat beside Amel on the sofa holding a large leather handbag on her lap. She wasn't what I considered beautiful, but she had a distinct look that made her look somewhat exotic. I guessed her to be in her late thirties. Her dark brown eyes travelled from mine down to my belly then back up again.

"Hello," I smiled looking from Amel to the woman. "I'm Octavia." I said extending my hand to the doctor.

"Nice to meet you Octavia," she said politely while shaking my hand. "I'm Doctor Rice, but you can call me Shayla."

"It's nice to meet you."

"How far along are you?" Shayla asked pointing to my stomach.

"Eight months," I said proudly.

"Almost at the finish line," Shayla smiled. "How wonderful."

"Yes," I said proudly. "Sometimes it feels like I'm being drug over the line."

"Your first one?" she asked.

"No, this is number two," I said. "And ten times more difficult than the first."

"You're carrying it beautifully," Shayla said. "Gorgeous...the joys of motherhood."

"Thank you. I'm very thankful," I said rubbing my belly. Shayla stared at me in silence for a moment with a look of euphoria on her face.

"Well, I should leave the two of you alone," Shayla finally said, standing with her bag in hand. "Amel take care of yourself, and next time be a little more careful on your food selection and drink plenty of water." She patted Amel on her hand and then turned to me. "Octavia it was a pleasure meeting you. Take care."

"Thank you for everything," I said courteously.

"Not a problem," she replied. She passed by me then walked out the door.

"You didn't have to come," Amel said in a hushed tone once we were alone. She sat up, and then pulled the towel from her head. "I really wish you hadn't."

"Of course I did, and sorry, but you know I had to check on you," I said, walking over to the sofa then sitting down. "Besides you *should* have stayed at home.

"I'm fine..." she said, "it turns out it was just something I ate. She gave me something for it and I feel ten times better now."

"Food poisoning?" I asked.

"Yeah…"Amel said nonchalantly. I had a nagging feeling that there was something Amel was leaving out.

"Is there anything else?" I questioned. *Silence.* "Amel?" I asked, looking at her.

"Dehydration," she said, looking at me with tears in her eyes. "That's all." I watched as a single tear fell from her eye down to her almond-colored cheek. "That's it…"

I knew that she was lying, but the last thing I wanted to do was push too hard. Since Amel's run in with drugs I was extra careful with how I dealt with her. There was always a part of me that was fearful that she would relapse. I knew it was wrong for me to assume that every time something went wrong with Amel that it would force her to slip back into substance abuse; after all, my own father was a recovered alcoholic and I had no concerns that he would return to his old habit. However, my feelings towards Amel were different for some strange reason.

"Well, why don't you go home," I said.

"I'm fine," she said.

"Amel go home," I said firmly. "That's a direct order." She looked at me, then finally nodded her head.

"Okay," she said.

"I'll walk you out," I offered, sliding off the sofa. I waited for her to gather her things together and then slip her feet into her designer pumps. We exited the office, and then walked in silence through the restaurant. Before we reached the front entrance Shayla stopped us.

"Octavia, the food here is fabulous," she purred. "I can't wait to come back."

"Thank you," I said, genuinely flattered. "My staff and I take pride in what we do."

"I can tell," she said politely. "Well, I better hit the ladies room before I get back to the office. Again, nice meeting you; and Amel don't forget what I told you about taking care of yourself. No one can watch out for *you* but *you*."

"That's true," I agreed, looking at Amel. She remained silent while nodding her head. Shayla smiled at each of us then walked away. I had parked my car upon arrival at the curb directly in front of the restaurant for easy access; I assumed Amel was parked in the normal employee parking lot. On a normal day I would have walked her to her vehicle considering that she wasn't feeling well, but I was trying to conserve some of my energy for when I returned home to Damon.

"Call me if you need me," I smiled before turning and giving her a big hug.

"I will. I'll see you Monday," she replied, pulling away from me slowly then walking away.

Once I was safely inside my vehicle I called my husband to inform him I was headed home and to give him the update on Amel's condition. As I prepared to pull my Benz onto the road I noticed Amel in my rearview mirror. She was standing on the sidewalk and appeared to be staring off into space. *What the hell?* I thought to myself. I shifted into park, waited until the traffic was clear, then opened my door and climbed out. I stepped back on to the sidewalk looking in Amel's direction.

"Amel," I called, "are you alright?" She turned her head redirecting her attention to me.

"Yes," she smiled. "I'm fine…just thinking"

"You can think at home," I teased.

"You're right."

"Good," I said in a serious manner. "Be careful."

"You be careful too," she said. "And thank you for everything Octavia." She waved her hand in the air before stepping off the sidewalk and into oncoming traffic. I stared in horror as I watched the tan SUV slam into her body, sending it soaring in midair.

"Noooo!" I screamed, moving as fast as I could to the scene of the accident.

"I didn't see her!" I heard the woman driver yell as she rushed out of her car. As I got closer to the place in the road where she was standing next to Amel's motionless body, I felt an all too familiar pain in my abdomen.

"Call 911!" someone yelled. I fought to maintain my balance as contraction after contraction rippled through my body. The scene became chaotic as passersby, and some of my customers, flooded the street. I watched as the driver of the car attempted to administer first aid to Amel. Her cheeks were flushed as tears poured from her eyes. I cried with her; unable to pull my eyes from the scene.

"Ughh," I groaned, clutching my belly. I felt a cooling sensation trickling down between my legs. My water had broken. *The baby is coming*, I thought.

"Amel!" I heard someone scream. "Oh…no…no!"

"Octavia!" Tabitha called, coming towards me. She was the first to notice me. "Are you okay?"

"My water broke," I informed her through clenched teeth. I tried to concentrate on my breathing; tried to calm my racing heart. My techniques were of no use.

"Doctor!" She called, waving her hand in the air. I looked up and saw Shayla coming in our direction. She ran to the place where we were standing with her handbag swinging from her arm.

"Are you okay?" she asked.

"Her water broke," Tabitha informed her. Shayla put her arm around me, allowing me to press my weight against her body.

"It's okay," she said, "I got you. Tabitha go check on the other employees." Tabitha nodded her head then ran off. I felt a sharp pain shooting through my arm as everything around me began to spin. "Let's get you to the hospital… now!" Shayla said. I nodded in agreement as everything slowly began to fade to black.

*****

I slipped in and out of consciousness while everything around me appeared in a blur. I could feel myself moving, hear the sound of tires screeching, and smell the distinct smell that only came with a new car. I was in the back of a vehicle. "I need you there immediately!" I heard a woman say before I passed out again. I can't tell you how many seconds passed, but I was later on my back with my legs up in stirrups, lying on a bed. The sounds and smells around me were notification that I was in the hospital.

"We've got to get her stabilized!" A man screamed. "This baby is coming now!"

"Damon," I said softly, attempting to fight against the weight bearing down on my eyes. I looked around at the figures surrounding me, wanting desperately to be able to make out the faces and distinguish between the voices.

"Who's Damon?" the man asked.

"Her husband," the woman replied.

"Something's wrong," I whispered. I felt heavy pressure in the center of my chest while in between my legs I felt hands, then the weight of what I knew was my child's head breaking through my gateway.

"It's a boy." I heard a soft hum, followed by the words, "We're losing her!"

I slipped between the gap of life and death; thoughts flooded my brain like raging rivers overtaking unprotected lands. I thought about my husband and the life the two of us shared, of my daughter and the joy she brings, of my parents and their unyielding love, of the baby I had just given birth to, and lastly of Shontay and the last moments of her life. I closed my eyes then took a deep excruciating breath, the one that was designated to be my last.

Chapter 3

Damon

I zoomed down Governor's Drive towards Huntsville Hospital, throwing all thought of speed and safety out the window. My only concern was to get to my wife because she needed me. My mind was racing from the things her employees had explained to me over the phone and with worry concerning Octavia's condition. I had given Octavia adequate time to get home when I decided to call and check on her. After receiving her voicemail twice, I called the restaurant. That's when Kaitlyn explained to me that something terrible had happened. She was hysterical, and her breathing was so shallow I was certain she was on the verge of hyperventilating. I was trying to make sense of her tear-filled babbling when Heather, another one of Octavia's employees, eventually took the phone from her and explained as calmly as I imagine was possible, that

Octavia was taken to the emergency room and that she had gone into labor after witnessing Amel get hit by a car.

"When?" I demanded, as I moved quickly exiting my home.

"I don't know," she stuttered. "About forty-five minutes ago."

"Why didn't anyone call me?" I snapped.

"We thought…we thought…Tabitha did." She sniffled. "I'm sorry. It's just crazy here right now. Amel is dead!" she cried erratically. I tried to remind myself that Octavia's employees were not the enemy and that my frustration was not directed at them, but more so caused by my concern for my wife.

"I'm sorry," I said as calmly as possible. "Do you know which hospital they took Octavia to?"

"No sir," she said softly.

"Thank you."

I ended the call, and then called the first reasonable and closest choice between the two main hospitals in the city. I was advised by the receptionist that a woman fitting my wife's description had been brought in earlier. As I drove to the hospital, I thought about what Octavia's employees disclosed to me about Amel. The thought of the conversation Octavia and I had earlier went through my mind. She thought that her nightmare about Gator had been some sort of omen of something terrible to come. It seemed she was right.

I maneuvered my Jaguar in the parking lot of the

Women's and Children center, slammed the gear into park, killed the engine, and then stepped out. I had left my home as soon as I found out what had taken place; however, I knew when the physician came out to speak with me in the waiting room that I was too late and something had gone horribly wrong. I listened in disbelief and regret as the middle-aged man of eastern decent, whom introduced himself as Doctor Aoura explained that Octavia had suffered a minor stroke after delivery; during which time, her heart stopped for a whole seven minutes. He advised me that she was now in a medically-induced coma as a precautionary measure to prevent damage to her brain.

Doctor Aoura stated that he was confident that Octavia would recover one hundred percent from the attack, but we wouldn't know for sure what damage, if any, had been caused until Octavia awakened. I couldn't understand how a woman as young and healthy as my wife could suffer a stroke, but then I reminded myself of all the stress and tragedy she had experienced. My wife had seen more death and destruction in four years than most people saw in a lifetime.

"What about the baby?" I asked.

"He didn't make it." he explained. "He was still born. I'm sorry for your loss Damon. You can see him when you're ready." I felt tears swelling in the wells of my eyes, but I commanded them to be still. I had to focus on Octavia, I had to be strong.

"I'd like to see my wife first," I said, clearing my throat.

"Understandable," he said, nodding his head.

*****

They say a man never knows what he has until it's gone. My thoughts alone of what my life would have been like without Octavia, lets me know that statement is true. I wished I had been with her when she was dealing with the loss of our son and going through the fight for her life; but to be honest, I don't know if I would have been able to handle it. The mere vision of Octavia flat lining on the operating table terrified me and shook me to my core. You have to understand that a portion of the fiber that makes me whole lies within Octavia, and it thrives with every breath she takes. If her breath—her life—were to ever be cut off, then so would mine. In essence, a part of me would die as well.

I stood by the metal bed staring at Octavia as she slept peacefully. I watched her chest as it rose and fell gently with every breath. Her brown sugar complexion glowed radiantly despite the things she had been through just hours before. I ran my fingertips from her wrist up the curve of her arm, thanking God for the blood that flowed through each and every one of her veins. I leaned down and kissed the top of her forehead. "I'll be back my love," I whispered. I turned and then exited the room headed for the morgue.

I had imagined several times how it would feel to hold my son in my arms. How he would wrap his tiny finger around mine, stare at me with honey-brown eyes like his mother, and how I would fall in love all over again. What I never imagined was that I would be looking down on his tiny, breathless body. I gently ran my hand across his head, stoking the fine black hairs with my fingertips and allowing the tears I fought so hard to keep under wraps to finally escape my eyes. I took a few minutes to get my emotions together then went to handle the paperwork associated with Octavia's admittance and our child's death. After contacting our parents, I returned to the Intensive Care Unit and the bed assigned to Octavia. I pushed the curtain back and found a tall, voluptuous sister standing next to the bed.

"Can I help you?" I asked, capturing her attention. The woman instantly turned on her heels, staring at me with dark—slanted brown eyes.

"I was just checking on her," she said almost mumbling. "How can I help you?" She stood by the bed with her heels planted firmly in a defensive stance, clutching her handbag close by her side, and looking as if she was prepared to battle at any moment.

"I'm her husband," I advised her.

There was a shift in her eyes and a change in her expression as her full lips turned up into a smile. "I'm sorry Damon," she exhaled. "You startled me."

"Who are you?" I questioned, wondering how she knew my name. I could tell by the dress and heels the woman wore that she was not a part of the staff and that her presence was clearly on a personal level.

"I'm Shayla Rice," she said to me. "I met Octavia

earlier at her restaurant. I was there when the accident took place and Octavia went into labor."

"How did you get in here?" I questioned. "The only visitors allowed to see my wife are her family." My protective nature instantly kicked in. I assumed she was a busy body looking for a story or gossip.

"I'm a doctor," she said. "I helped administer aid to Octavia and drove her to the hospital."

"Thank you," I said, slowly letting down my guard.

"I was happy to help and I'm sorry for invading your privacy," she said. "I had an emergency page of my own after I got her here, so I left, but I was just so concerned about her and your child." The mere mention of my son caused a knot to develop in my stomach.

"How is the baby?" Shayla asked brightly. "Did she have a girl or a boy?"

"A boy," I informed her. "However, he didn't make it."

"Oh my," she said, throwing her hand against her chest. "She was so happy…I'm so sorry Damon."

"Thank you," I said. There was a moment of silence between the two of us until Shayla finally stated she was leaving.

"Thank you again for what you did," I said. "I sincerely appreciate it."

"It was truly my pleasure," she said, looking at me. "Take care."

Chapter 4

Octavia

I blinked once, then once more, adjusting my eyes to the soft fluorescent lights beaming down upon me in the bed. The inside of my mouth felt like it had been scrubbed raw. I flinched as I swallowed, wanting desperately to saturate my painfully dry throat. Looking over to my right, I saw my husband asleep on the small leather recliner next to the bed. He was stretched out with his mouth hanging slightly open, wearing the uncommon attire of a t-shirt, sweat pants and *Nikes*. I cut my eyes from one side of the room to the other admiring the wall-to-wall flowers; from roses to calla lilies, the room was covered. I smiled knowing that my husband was responsible for the majority of my little-personal garden.

"Damon," I spoke aloud, barley recognizing my own voice. I watched him as he tossed then turned in the chair looking extremely uncomfortable. "Damon," I called again, this time slightly louder. His eyes opened instantly. He stared at me like he was looking at me for the first time.

"Hey," I said smiling.

"Hey baby." he said sitting up. "I thought I was dreaming." He climbed out the chair he was sitting in and walked over and stood next to the bed I was in. "How do you feel?"

"Thirsty," I sighed.

"Let me get you some water," he said quickly. He moved to the small plastic canister sitting on the metal, rolling tray in the corner of the room and began to fill up one of the plastic cups resting on the tray.

"Here you go," he said, returning to my bedside. My body felt extremely heavy as I sat up with Damon's assistance. "Drink slow," he instructed, cradling the back of my head with one hand and holding the cup to my lips with the other. The water tasted like the best thing I had ever had as it cooled my tingling tongue, then coated my aching throat. I took another small sip before reclining back in the bed.

"Thank you," I said appreciatively.

"No thank you is ever needed," he replied. He sat the cup down on the nightstand beside the bed then leaned over and kissed my cheek. "I missed you."

"How long have I been out?" I asked. "A couple of hours?"

"Three days," Damon informed me.

"Three days…" I said in disbelief.

"Yes," he said. "Do you remember how you got here?" I paused, attempting to focus and think back. My memories slowly began to resurface.

"My water broke," I said slowly. "I was standing in the street outside the restaurant. Tabitha came to help and one of my customers—"

"Shayla?" Damon asked, cutting me off.

I remembered the woman whom had helped me and Amel. "Yes," I answered. "She was there, but then it gets foggy. They said the baby was a boy and…I remember the pain in my chest and I felt like I was dying. My life flashed before me…" I paused while trying to remember why I was in the middle of the street in the first place. The vision of Amel lying dead on the pavement danced vividly before me. "Amel," I breathed. I felt a small lump rising in my throat. "She walked out…in front of the car…she just stepped off the sidewalk into traffic…it was horrible…seeing her body—"

"Shhh…" Damon ordered, brushing my hair with the palm of his hand. "Don't think about that right now."

I nodded my head as tears trickled down my cheeks. I wanted to understand what made Amel do what she did. I wanted to try and make sense of it, but I couldn't. I wished that I could flip the scene and create a new canvas of the picture of her intentionally stepping off the curb that day, but no amount of imagination, no degree of wishful thinking could undo that memory. Maybe, she slipped and I missed interpreted her actions. I thought

I had seen it exactly as it had taken place, but maybe I was wrong. It didn't make sense. I inhaled through my nose then slowly exhaled through my parted lips telling myself that I had to focus on the positive in that moment; the newest addition to my family. I assumed due to my extended rest our son was in the nursery. Something I never imagined Damon would allow, but I presumed he felt it necessary.

"You got what you wanted," I said, forcing myself to look on the brighter side.

"What's that sweetie?" Damon asked, stroking my cheek with his fingertips.

"A boy," I answered. *Silence.* He stopped caressing my face then stood up straight. I stared at him, searching his eyes with mine waiting for him to respond. He didn't. There was something in Damon's expression that ignited the flames of my worst fears; the fear of losing a child. I looked around the room again. I had noticed the flowers earlier, but I had failed to realize, there was nothing in the room indicating the celebration of the birth of our son. "Damon?" I asked, hoping that my perception was wrong. He had sympathy in his eyes as he shook his head.

"I'm sorry," he said gently. "He didn't make it."

"What?" The small lump that had developed in my throat earlier as I thought of Amel, resurfaced; this time feeling like a melon blocking the entrance of my airway. "Dame—" I whispered, almost breathless.

"I'm so sorry Octavia," he said compassionately. "I thought they told you…"

I covered my lips with one hand while shaking my head. "Noooo…" I sobbed loudly. "Whyyy!"

"It's okay, "Damon whispered.

"What did I do wrong?" I whined; crying hysterically. "Why?" Damon eased down on the bed then stretched out next to me.

"You didn't do anything wrong," he said, pulling me into his arms. I lay with my head on his chest and tears falling freely from my eyes, saturating his t-shirt.

"What happened?" I asked. I listened as Damon gave me the same explanation provided to him by the doctor and the things that transpired during the delivery. "I did this…" I said somberly. "The stress and the pressure… you told me…you told me to slow down! But I didn't…I just kept going and going and…"

"No," Damon said firmly. "Listen to me…this was not your fault Octavia. Don't you dare blame yourself. There was nothing you could do, so don't think like that bae."

I heard his words, but I couldn't help thinking that I could have done things differently. I should have rested more. I should have focused on our child rather than trying to be there for everyone else. I felt enormous guilt as I closed my eyes, allowing my sorrow and my tears to overflow. I cried until my eyes were swollen and the tears would no longer come.

The on-call physician came to check my vitals then Damon assisted me into a wheelchair and pushed me to the hospital morgue. I sat in the wheelchair, with

Damon standing behind me, while looking down at our son. I asked myself why I felt so detached from the baby I had wanted so badly just days earlier. I had never lost a child before, but one thing I was sure of was that even through death, a mother's love flows fluently and vibrantly and the bond is undeniable. I, however, felt empty and shallow.

"Let's go," I said to Damon. "I've seen enough."

Chapter 5

Damon

*H*aving to break the news to Octavia about our son was one of the hardest things I had yet to do in my life. I hated seeing her in so much pain, pain that I wanted desperately to ease but I couldn't. I wished a thousand times or more that I was capable of undoing what had taken place, but the reality of it all is that no matter how much money or how much power we possess, there are still some things that are out of our hands. I understood that, but it didn't mean that I was not willing to fight with all my might to help her get through her time of mourning. Octavia was cleared for release from the hospital seventy-two hours after she woke from the coma. And after multiple testing, I was happy to hear that there was no permanent physical damage to her body. The neurologist who came in to examine her advised us that Octavia's brain functions and the patterns of the test showed no indication of disruption. It was as if my wife had never even had the stroke in the first place. The physicians stated she was lucky, I knew the truth was she was blessed and the epitome of a survivor.

I knew Octavia's emotional scarring was a different matter; however, I was willing to help, as best I could, her overcome and heal. During Octavia's stay at the hospital, I remained by her bedside, only leaving to check in on Jasmine, who was in my in-law's care, and to bury our son. I held back on burying our baby until Octavia recovered from her medical coma, because I felt it was only right to give her the opportunity to see him laid to rest. I was slightly surprised when she refused the offer.

"Please just take care of it," she said.

I honored her request by having a graveside service for our child, whom I given the name the two of us had originally chosen in the event that she gave birth to a son; Josiah Savoy Whitmore. The service was held in Valhalla Memory Gardens; sadly it was the same graveyard where we laid Savoy and Shontay to rest. I took solace that someday, I would see each of them again and I hoped it would be that we all would celebrate in Paradise. Octavia requested that I pick up a few things from her office so that she could play catch up on what she'd been missing. I swung by the Ambiance 2 first, just so that I could commend the staff of the job they were doing, then I headed to the Ambiance. I'll admit, I was impressed with the way Octavia's crews at both her locations seem to work together like a well-oiled machine and how they

appeared to be handling the loss of one of their own;
Amel. Although, I had advised Tabitha and the other
employees to call me if they experienced any problems
or had any questions, I hadn't received so much as a text.
It was obvious that Octavia had prepared and trained
them well.

The tragedy that had taken place in front of the
Ambiance had no visible effect on business. As usual
the dining room was packed and the customers seemed
oblivious to the chaos that had taken place almost a
week before. I was beginning to think that all of the
drama associated with my family was somewhat of an
attraction for others. After the incident where Kenny and
Donna were murdered at the Ambiance 2, I was certain
that business would die before the restaurant even had
a chance. But on the contrary, Octavia said her profits
had exceeded her projected plans and all expectations.
I nodded my head acknowledging the tall, red head
standing behind the hostess booth before heading in
the direction of the office. I could hear a female voice
speaking loudly as I approached Octavia's office door,
and from the elevated tone and her choice of words, I
knew that the conversation she was having was not a
pleasant one. I tapped on the door then waited patiently.

"One moment!" she said loudly. "I can't believe this!"
she blurted. "You can't be serious. Where does that
leave me? You're asking for too much!" I felt slightly
uncomfortable for eavesdropping on the conversation,
but at the same time I was on a mission and business had

to be handled. I knocked again.

"I said give me a fucking moment!" she snapped. There was aggravation and anger in her voice. I turned the door handle, then pushed the door open. "Did you not hear what I just—" Tabitha immediately halted her rant when she saw that I was the one who had interrupted her. I hadn't recognized her voice from outside, and to be honest, I was surprised that she was the one having an obvious temper tantrum on the phone. I hadn't had a lot of interaction with Octavia's employees, but the times I had come across Tabitha, she took me as mild and timid. The woman standing before me now appeared to be the exact opposite. She stood with one hand planted firmly on her hip and the other holding a cell phone to her ear. Her skin looked slightly pale as she stared at me with wide eyes.

"Your moment is up," I said firmly.

"I have to go," she said, speaking into the phone. She quickly pressed a button on her device then sat it down on the edge of the desk. "Damon...I'm sorry...I wasn't expecting you." She said. I watched as she tugged on the hem of the short suit jacket she was wearing then smoothed her hands down the front of the matching pants. "I'm sorry. How is Octavia?"

"I'm actually on my way to pick her up. Her doctor finally gave the approval for her to come home." I stepped inside the office and shut the door behind me.

"That's...that's great," she said, fidgeting with her nails. "We miss her around here...things haven't been the same without her." She gave me a slight smile.

"I'm sure they haven't," I said.

"Octavia is a great person. She's easy to love and naturally her presence would be missed."

"That she is," I agreed. I loved talking about my wife, but I also felt it necessary to address other issues with Tabitha at that moment like the phone call which clearly had her in disarray. "Is everything alright with you?" I questioned.

"Everything is fine," she said. "My boyfriend and I just had a fight; that's all." Tabitha looked at me then at the floor before looking at me again. "I'm embarrassed that you heard that."

"Every relationship has its moments," I said. "But we have to learn how to separate business from personal... especially when we work for someone else." It was clear that she was uncomfortable and so she should be. I appreciated the fact that she was handling the majority of the business in Octavia's absence, but the truth was, she was getting paid to do so and along with her pay came certain expectations; such as leaving her personal issues—and it was clear she had some—at home. I had a major problem with the display of unprofessionalism I overheard before I opened the door. There is a time and place for everything; however, my wife's office was not the place.

"I want to first thank you for everything you're doing," I began. "I know the past few days have been difficult for everyone and you've stepped up, taking additional responsibilities and hours."

"They haven't been that bad," she said quickly. "And of course I did. We were short staffed, it's my job to do so."

"You were not only short staffed," I reminded her. "You lost one of your cohorts. Octavia's told me how close knit the members of her teams are. "

"Amel will be missed," she said, casually. "But I think we both know that life goes on. Death is something we all must face."

"This is true," I said, slightly concerned by her nonchalant attitude.

"I was in shock at first," she continued, as if reading my mind, "but again, life *and* business must go on."

I nodded my head. "Speaking of business," I said. "Before you discovered it was me at the door, you were using language that I deem inappropriate." The confidence Tabitha displayed seconds earlier vanished. She once again looked worried. "I'm sure if Octavia was here she would also find your choice of words inappropriate. What if a customer was at the door instead of me? What if it was a vendor at the door looking to establish a business relationship with Octavia?" I waited for her response.

"I thought it was one of the employees," she said, nervously.

"You didn't think," I declared. "If you had of thought, the two of us would not be having this conversation. The first step in being a great leader is knowing how and when to communicate."

"I'm sorry," she said. "You're right. It won't happen again."

"I'm glad." I said. "So, how's business?"

"Great," she said. "The numbers look good for today, last I checked we were already at a little over three thousand."

"Not bad," I said. "Not bad at all."

"I try," she said with a smile. It was clear she was proud of what the restaurant had accomplished and I could understand why. I had Tabitha gather the reports Octavia had requested then I prepared to leave.

"Tabitha…one question," I asked, stopping at the door.

"What's that?"

"What happened the day Amel was killed?"

"I don't know," she said, shrugging her shoulders. "I was in the dining room when I heard the commotion outside. When I came out I saw Amel had been hit and that's when I spotted Octavia hunched over clutching her belly. I ran up to her and that's when the doctor—"

"Shayla," I stated.

"Yes, Shayla came up and told me she would further assist. After that, I just kinda freaked out. I sat in the bathroom hysterical."

"I see," I said, observing her carefully. "Well, thank you." I exited the office while thinking to myself that something about her just wasn't right.

*****

I exited the interstate in the direction of my home while Octavia sat in the passenger seat relaxing against the soft leather and staring out the window. She wore a sleeveless yellow silk summer dress that stopped just above her knees and yellow sandals; her naturally curly hair pulled back in a simple, but classy ponytail. She wore no makeup and the truth is she didn't need to; Octavia is a natural beauty that needed no additives.

"How are you feeling?" I asked. She pulled her gaze from the window then turned to look at me.

"Okay," she said, smiling slightly. "Happy to be headed home."

"That makes two of us," I said.

"You didn't have to stay with me," she said softly. "I would have been fine."

"I did have to stay," I said. I reached over then took her hand in mine while keeping my eyes on the road ahead. "There was nowhere I would have rather been." I lifted the back of her hand to my lips then gave it a tender kiss. Octavia smiled then returned to looking out the window. The two of us rode in silence with or fingers intertwined.

"How were things at the restaurants?" she asked.

"Things were good," I said honestly. "Marilyn is doing her thing at the Ambiance 2 and Tabitha seems to be maintaining at the Ambiance."

"I'll have to find a replacement for Amel," she said solemnly. "I never thought I would have to do so like this. Maybe it's time I move Tabitha up."

"Don't make any rush decisions," I suggested. "I think you should give it some time and see how things play out in the next few weeks."

"Why?" Octavia asked, frowning as she looked at me. "Did something happen?"

"Nothing happened," I said, not wanting her to worry. "I just think you should see how she handles things. You never want to make a decision based solely on your current emotions." I didn't want to alarm Octavia of the behavior Tabitha had displayed when I stopped by the restaurant. I knew if I had she would insist on returning to work immediately and quite possibly before she was ready.

"You're right," she agreed.

I pulled up to the gate leading to our home, entered the security code on the keypad, and then waited for the gate to open before proceeding through. Octavia's father's F150 was parked in the front of our home along with my mother's Mercedes.

"The gangs all here," she said as I pulled around our circular driveway, parking behind my mother's car.

"It's not too much. Is it?" I asked, slightly uneasy. I had originally planned a quiet homecoming for Octavia, that would include just me and our daughter, but our mothers insisted that what Octavia needed was to be surrounded by family and those that loved her the most. My father and Octavia's father felt that she needed rest and time to settle in. However, the vote was two very determined mothers against three men, and when it comes to the laws of nature, a mother's determination can shake down the strongest of men.

"Of course not," she said.

"Good," I exhaled. "Because I couldn't keep them away even if I wanted to. Mama and Charlene weren't having it."

"Trust me I understand," she said. "My mother is a force of nature by herself. Combine that with the designer diva, aka Ilene, and you've got hell surrounded by ten gallons of gasoline and three lit matches." We both laughed. It felt good hearing my wife laugh again. I got out the car then walked around to the passenger's side and held the door open for her. A second later our front door flew open and Jasmine came bouncing down the front steps, dragging my mother behind her. Charlene, Charles and my father Damon Sr. followed behind them. My baby girl wore a pretty yellow dress and a pair of matching yellow sandals. The expression of happiness scrolled across her little face made it evident that she had missed her mother.

"Mommy!" Jasmine sung. Her curly pigtails flapped in the wind as she ran up, greeting Octavia.

"Hey pretty girl!" Octavia smiled, kneeling down to eye level with our daughter. "I missed you!"

"I miss you too Mommy," Jasmine smiled brightly. She wrapped her arms around her mother's neck as Octavia slowly lifted her off the ground and up around her waist. The two of them shared a hug and several kisses until Octavia finally eased Jasmine back on the ground. I watched as each of our parents greeted and extended their open arms to Octavia, each one telling her how much they loved her and were happy to have her home. Octavia smiled and laughed and smiled some more; I was beginning to think that our mothers were right. Maybe returning to our norm was the answer to Octavia's emotional healing.

*****

I pushed back from the dining room table then exhaled while staring at the empty plate on the table in front t of me. After enjoying the home-cooked meal Charlene had prepared, I was full and almost positive I had gained five pounds. My mother-in-law had gone all out with the spread, preparing smoked turkey, dressing, turnip greens, potato salad, a yam casserole, and rolls. The meal made it feel like Thanksgiving in May, and I was happier than a kid on Christmas. Octavia sat on one side of me at the table while my mother sat on the other. I noticed Octavia had barely touched her food. In the hospital she blamed her loss of appetite on the food selection. Now, I was hoping that I would see that change.

"You okay babe?" I asked, watching her carefully.

"I'm fine," she said, flashing her eyes at me. "Just a little tired. I think I'll go upstairs and lay down for a little while."

"Okay," I said. "You need some help?"

"No, but thank you," she said as she rose from the

table. She smiled while looking around the table. "I'm going to go take a nap," she announced. She leaned down and kissed Jasmine on the top of her head before saying her goodbyes and exiting the dining room. After we all watched her leave the room, the conversations going on at the table continued. I listened as my father and Charles went back and forth discussing the current state of the *NBA* and who they thought were the most influential leaders in the league while Charlene entertained Jasmine.

"How are you darling?" Mama asked looking at me.

"I'm good," I answered. "How are you?"

"Fabulous," she sighed.

"How's Donovan?" I questioned, thinking about my nephew. It was still hard for me to believe that my mother and father had taken on the task to raise another child. Don't get me wrong, it's not because I thought the feat was too great for them, but my mother was a social diva in every sense of the word and in my opinion raising another child would cramp her style. However, in the year and a half that Donovan had been in her and my father's custody, she seemed to be balancing it all without a sweat or worry.

"Donovan is perfect," she sighed, "Another fine Whitmore man in training."

"Why didn't you bring him with you?"

"Your father felt it best that we not overwhelm Octavia right now," she informed me. "Plus, he has pre-K basketball camp for the summer and today he had practice. So, I left him in Isabella's care."

"When Octavia feels up to it, I'll have to come get him for the weekend," I suggested. "Give you and Pops a break."

"Sounds good darling," Mama smiled. "But do you think you can also take Odessa? In fact she's one you can keep...*forever*! I'll even pay you. Just name your price." I looked down the table at my father to see if he had heard my mother's comment. He continued to laugh and debate with Charles. Charlene had also taken part in their conversation.

"How is Grandma," I asked.

"She's still kicking," Mama said smirking. "Unfortunately." She whispered. It was obvious that the rift between my grandmother and mother was still present, despite my parents now being my grandmother's caregivers as well. I had come to the conclusion that there were some women who would forever be at odds. My mother and grandmother were two of them.

"Well, send her my love," I said, shaking my head.

"What about my offer darling?" Mama asked. The expression on her face let me know that she was dead ass serious about her invitation for me to take grandma off her hands. If I was a single man I might have taken her up on her offer, at no cost of course; but there was no way in hell Octavia was going for it. My grandmother tried in no way to hide the fact that she disliked the choice I made when marrying Octavia; and Octavia tried in no way to hide the fact that she didn't give a damn. In a perfect world all of the women in my life would get along, hold hands, and have tea or at least get drunk together, but the reality of it all was that if I wanted to keep the peace and harmony, I had to keep them separated.

"I'll pass," I finally answered.

"Very well," mama said, waving her hand in the air. "Remember I offered."

"I'll do that," I chuckled.

"Who wants dessert?" Charlene called from the other end of the table. Jasmine was the first to raise her hand, followed by her two grandfathers providing their answers verbally.

"Not me," I said politely. "I'm still full from the main course."

"You have got to make room for pie," Charlene insisted, standing up. "It's pecan and your mother made it."

"Really?" I asked. I was surprised and slightly terrified of the thought. I had never seen my mama bake anything. In fact, I didn't even know she could bake!

"Of course not dear. Don't be absurd," Mama laughed lightly. "Courtesy of Isabella."

"I thought you said you did it," Charlene frowned.

"I said I was bringing a homemade pie," Mama rebutted, rising from her chair. "And I did. I didn't say I made it." She patted me on my shoulders then walked in Charlene's direction. "Charlene darling, you should know me so much better than that."

"I was hoping you would surprise me," Charlene laughed. Jasmine instantly climbed off her chair and followed the two women as they exited the dining room towards the kitchen. I loved the friendship that was now shared between my mother and Charlene. My mother was a woman of few friends and many fake associates. It was good to see another woman outside of Octavia and Isabella who accepted her and genuinely cared about her. As soon as the women and my daughter were out of ear shot, the conversation changed between my father-in-law and my father.

"Did you catch the morning news?" Charles asked me.

"No," I admitted. "What I miss?"

"Clint Harvey is missing," Charles informed me.

"Gator's attorney?" I asked.

"Yes," Charles said. "According to reports, he hasn't been to work in three days. They went to his home and his car was parked in the driveway, but there's no sign of the man. It's like he disappeared off the face of the earth."

"You think Gator had something to do with it?" I questioned.

"I don't know," Charles said. "Why would he?"

"He did lose the case," I reminded him. "One that I'm sure he was compensated quit well for taking in the first place."

"Yeah, but why knock off the person responsible for your appeal? Charles questioned. "That doesn't make sense. Why not the judge that convicted him?"

"Or the jury," my father added. "And why wait months

after the trial is over? Gator doesn't seem like that type."

I agreed with my father. Gator wasn't the type. He was more of the type to come up with a solution before there was a problem.

"Exactly," Charles said with a frown on his face. "I don't think this is the work of Gator."

"Maybe Clint was involved in some other dealings," I suggested.

"Maybe," Charles said. "Or he could be taking a personal hiatus…either way; something tells me this is going to lead to some interesting events."

"With ties to Gator, I wouldn't expect any less." I said.

*****

My parents and in-laws were a fine example of family and love. After dinner and desert, Charlene and my mother cleaned the kitchen while I got caught up on me and Octavia's laundry. Charles and my father were responsible for keeping Jasmine entertained, which in its self was a full-time job. At three and a half years old, Jasmine was a walking, talking, bundle of energy with an abundance of questions. Although I felt my daughter was wise beyond her years, I was happy she was not at the point yet where she could comprehend the difference between life and death.

When I explained to Jasmine that we weren't going to bring home the new baby and that her little brother had died, I expected her to be confused or ask questions why. She never did. Instead she said, "Okay daddy" and walked away without further discussion. I excused myself from the laundry to go check on Octavia. I found her stretched across our bed, looking like sleeping beauty awaiting a kiss from her king. I chose not to disturb her, closing the door then heading back downstairs. After my parents left, I gave Jasmine a bath then slipped her pink princess gown over her head before tucking her in bed.

"I want Mommy," she said, staring at me with the big brown eyes.

"Mommy can tuck you in tomorrow," I said. "She's sleeping—"

"I'm up now," Octavia said from behind me. I turned around and found her standing in the doorway of Jasmine's bedroom.

"Looks like you're in luck munchkin," I said, kissing my daughter's cheek. "Daddy loves you."

"I love you," Jasmine said sweetly.

I walked up to Octavia and then kissed her cheek. "I love you," I said.

"I love you more," she replied.

*****

I stretched my arms out across the bed, searching for Octavia's body, only to discover her side of the bed was empty. 1:37 stood out in bright red numbers on my alarm clock. I tossed the covers back then eased out of bed, stepping onto the carpeted floor. My first stop was by Jasmine's bedroom. I assumed Jasmine may have gotten up in the middle of the night and Octavia had gone to check in on her. I found Jasmine alone, fast asleep, clutching one of her stuffed bears in between her arms. I closed the door to Jasmine's room, preparing to head downstairs, when I heard music coming from the bedroom across the hall. The room that Octavia and I had designated as the nursery.

I stepped barefoot across the hall then pushed the door open. The small carousel that was attached to the wooden crib moved slowly while the soft sounds of a lullaby flowed through the speaker. Octavia sat on the window seat with her knees pulled up to her chest, her hands covering her face; she was weeping softly. I wanted to say something to her, anything that would be of comfort, but there were no words that I could recite that I hadn't already. I chose not to speak. I reached down, lifting her up in my arms. She wrapped her arms around my neck, allowing her warm tears to trickle down my neck on to my bare chest. I carried Octavia back into our bedroom, and then eased her down on top of the bed. I settled in behind her and then cradled her in my arms; securing her in my embrace. Octavia's crying continued as she wrapped her arms around my biceps. My heart ached because my love was in pain; a pain that I had no way of easing. There is no worst feeling than knowing the woman you love is hurting, and there is nothing you can do about it. I buried my face in her hair as my own tears trickled from my eyes.

Chapter 6

Damon

Four weeks later

"Yes, I'm sure," Octavia repeated, filling my glass with orange juice. I was pleasantly surprised when I came down stairs to find breakfast waiting on the table and my wife wearing a suit and heels. Her hair hung loosely over her shoulders and she looked ready to take on the world. Jasmine was also dressed in denim shorts, a hot pink t-shirt, and clean white sneakers with her hair separated into two ponytails. When I asked my wife where she was going, she proudly announced that she was going to work, I was going to my office, and Jasmine was going to daycare. I reminded her we had a home office for both of our convenience.

"I can work right here," I said.

"You need to be back in the middle of the action. Besides, I'm sure there are several investors just waiting for your expertise," she said. "I need to get back on my grind, and Jasmine needs to be around children her own age." I'd asked her if she was sure at least three times and each time her answer was the same, "Yes, I'm sure. I'm fine."

"My only concern is you and our daughter," I told her. "Everything and everyone else can wait." I dug my fork in the omelet resting on the plate on the table before me. "This is good," I said, momentarily distracted from the subject at hand.

"Your favorite: ham, mushrooms, cheddar, and to-matoes," Octavia sang. She opened the refrigerator door then sat the glass pitcher containing the juice back on the shelf. "Oh, and tonight I was thinking rib eye steaks, loaded baked potatoes, fresh crescent rolls, and string green beans... Maybe I'll bring home a nice slice of my "Better than Sex" chocolate cheesecake from the restaurant." It was obvious my love was using food to persuade me. I took another bite of my omelet while staring at her.

"Okay," I finally agreed. It was obvious her persuasion had worked. "But if at any time you feel that you need me. Call me immediately."

"I will," she said happily.

"No, I want to hear the words," I said sternly.

"I promise Damon," she sighed, shaking her head. "When did you become such a worrier?"

"The moment I realized what I have," I said. "And I'm not a worrier, I'm your man. It's my job to protect you."

She smiled seductively while walking over to the table. "You do a very good job of it," she said. "And I love you for it." She cradled my face in her hands then pressed her lips to mine. Her warm tongue greeted mine with passion and force. In my pants my man stood at attention, ready for action.

"Stop it," I ordered, pulling away. "You know Ms. Kitty hasn't been given permission to play."

"What I have planned for you doesn't require Ms. Kitty," she said suggestively. She flicked her tongue out then across her bottom lip. I felt my soldier leap with anticipation.

"Don't start woman," I said casually.

"Jasmine baby, why don't you go in the living room," she said, looking at our daughter. "You left baby doll in there all alone. Play with her until Mommy comes to get you."

"She's not scared," Jasmine said. She continued to sit at the table kicking her legs.

I laughed. "I told you she was wise beyond her years and curious."

Octavia shook her head then walked over to the kitchen island where her handbag was sitting. She pulled out ten dollars and extended it to Jasmine.

"Thank you," Jasmine giggled, hopping down off the chair. She ran out the kitchen in the direction of our family room.

"That's why her bank is so fat," I teased. "You bribe my baby...so you can be nasty!"

"Umm, hum and you like it," she said, extending her hand to me. I allowed her to lead me to the walk-in pantry in the corner of the room. I could see the family room where Jasmine was now playing, but still had enough time to cease and desist without Octavia and me getting caught. Octavia smiled seductively as she eased down on her knees inside the pantry. "Did he miss me?" she asked. She grabbed the waistband of my basketball shorts and then pulled them down around my ankles. My dick stood up like a beacon in the night, leading the way home. "I guess that means yes!" she laughed slyly.

"You got jokes," I said. "We'll see how many laughs I get when I get the chance—" My words were halted by the warm, wet feel of her lips wrapping around my dick. "Damn..." I moaned.

Octavia slowly sucked my lower head while rolling her tongue back and forth. The sound of her lips popping as she inched closer and closer to the base of my dick caused it to swell even more. She pulled me from her lips then licked up then down and finally around my head before plunging down on my pole and giving me free reign to her throat. My knees shook as she bobbed up and down, and up and down again, then shook her head back and forth making my dick jump in her mouth. "Yes!" I moaned, grabbing a hand full of her hair. My heart began to beat quickly as Octavia moved her lips to my sack and started to suck it gently. I stared in her honey-brown eyes watching as she released my sack then returned to my rock-hard pole. She plunged down again then came back up, concentrating on my head. She locked her lips around my man, rotating her tongue around and around and around until the muscles in my thighs and stomach constricted almost to the point of being unbearable.

"Here it comes…" I moaned. "Here it comes…" My heart felt like it was in a marathon; racing to the finish line as I closed my eyes and released my liquid buildup. Octavia held me in between her jaws until I was deflated; then she swallowed, and took me in her mouth again.

"Shit!" I yelled, flinching from the tingling sensation.

"Daddy?" Jasmine called. I quickly pulled the pantry doors closed. Octavia continued to clutch me in between her lips.

"Da…dad…dy's…coming baby," I heaved, attempting to pull away from Octavia's grasp. "Stop it!" I whispered to Octavia.

"Where are you?" Jasmine called. A minute later, I heard a small tap on the pantry door. I quickly pushed Octavia away, and pulled up my shorts. Octavia covered her mouth in an attempt to muffle her laugh.

"Daddy? Mommy? Are you praying…?"

"No, baby, why?" Octavia asked.

"Why are you on the floor?" Jasmine asked innocently.

"Daddy was praying and I was helping to answer his prayers." Octavia said, rising to her feet.

"Oh," Jasmine said. "Why Daddy not on his knees then?"

"Why 'isn't' Daddy on his knees," Octavia corrected

her. "And soon he will be. In fact, Daddy normally stays on his knees daily. How do you think we got you?" Octavia grinned looking at me.

"You're bad," I whispered, chuckling.

"And you love it," she said.

"That I do," I said before opening the pantry doors and stepping out. Jasmine stood with her eyes wide, holding her doll in her hands. "Hey munchkin," I smiled, lifting her up into my arms.

"Did you get what you asked for?" Jasmine asked curiously.

"That and then some," I said, looking back at Octavia. She winked her eye, and then left the room.

*****

My employees were in full swing when I finally made it to my office and I was still on a natural high from the head job my wife had given me an hour earlier. After thanking everyone for their concern in regards to Octavia, I went to my office, closed the door and went to work. I was not only thankful, but impressed by how well my team had managed in my absence. I still had an abundance of messages, but the important thing was that there were no major issues and we were still turning a profit. I was replaying my voicemail messages when I stumbled one that caught my attention.

"Damon, this is Clint Harvey; call me at 256-555-5987 when you get this message. I'm thinking of investing in a few businesses and I need some professional advice."

The message was left around the time that I had been gone from the office to tend to Octavia during her stay at the hospital. I called the number Clint left on my voicemail only to discover his number was no longer in service. I made another call, this time to Charles.

"What's going on son?" Charles answered.

"Clint Harvey called me," I explained.

"What did he want?"

"He said he was looking to invest."

"When was this?"

"It was four weeks ago," I said. "I'm just now checking my messages and when I called the number back it said the number is out of service."

"What do you think he really wanted?" Charles asked from the other end of the phone.

"I don't know," I said truthfully. "I haven't seen the man since the trial and the two of us didn't say as much as 'hello' even then."

"You want me to make a few calls?" Charles asked. "See if any of my old buddies has heard anything?"

Charles was referring to his comrades that he once associated with when he was an active private investigator. Any time Charles called in a favor, information was provided if there was some to be found.

"Do that please," I said. Two hours later Charles called me back.

"As it turns out your boy Clint has been seen," he informed me.

"Really? Where?"

"Vacationing on the islands of St. Maarten."

"Spending the money he earned from Gator," I said. "Maybe he really did need my professional advice."

"Maybe," Charles said. "I now know why his number is no longer in service."

"Why is that?"

"When he was spotted he wasn't alone." Charles said. "He was in the company of a Mrs. Diamond Douglass, aka, Gator's wife; and sources say the two of them looked quit cozy."

"So that's the reason Clint's on the run," I stated.

"To be honest, I don't think he has any reason to be alarmed," Charles said. "Gator's behind bars, his organization is almost obsolete, and his associates are probably happy he's on lock so they can take the lead. Not to mention, it's clear he doesn't have his wife's loyalty."

"That's true," I said. "Well, now we know."

"That we do son," Charles said.

Chapter 7

Octavia

On the outside I looked fine; my body was quickly returning to its form and shape before my pregnancy, but inside I still felt dull like there was something missing or as if an unknown force were reaching out to me. A force, that at times felt like it was stronger than everything I had inside of me, and that at any second it might overpower me and everything that makes me who I am would be lost. I knew I had to move on and regain my inner power and one of the best ways for me to actually do so was for me to get up and get moving. I had to for the sake of my husband, my daughter, and most importantly…my sanity.

I decided my first step would be returning to work. My employees greeted me with open arms and an abundance of "Welcome backs" as I made my rounds throughout the building, taking the time to converse with each one of them and let them know how much they were appreciated. My spirits were instantly lifted just by being in the midst of the lively group of men and women that made up my team. I hadn't seen Tabitha on the floor, so I assumed she was in my office; when I turned the handle and opened the door, I discovered I was right. I wasn't, however, prepared for what my eyes stumbled upon. She sat in my chair with her back to the door while talking on the phone. She was reclining comfortably in the leather high back and had the nerve to have her feet propped up against my office wall! It was clear to me from the laughter in her voice that she was enjoying her conversation. I stepped inside the room, then pushed on the door closed, causing it to slam.

"Hold on," she said to the person on the other end. She dropped her feet from their elevated position and spun around in the chair; looking at me. "Octavia!" she said quickly. She hopped up; smoothing her hands over the front of the fitted jacket and skirt she wore.

"Good Morning," I said, walking up to the desk. I sat my handbag on the edge along with my keys, while giving Tabitha a look that said, "Step aside." I received confirmation that she got the message when she hauled ass moving from behind my desk.

"Good Morning," she said. She didn't bother saying anything to her caller and instead pressed a button, I assumed to end the call. There was a change in her appearance, and not just in her choice of attire, which had not been approved by me nor my husband, but her normally natural skin was now adorned with bold makeup and her blond hair was highlighted with warm shades of red. She looked nice, I won't deny that, but it was totally unexpected.

"Did I disturb you?" I asked, walking around the desk and then sitting down in the chair.

"Of course not boss," she said nervously. "You could never disturb me. I'm surprised to see you back so soon."

"I felt it was necessary," I said staring at her. *Obviously, my feelings were justified,* I thought.

"Well, I think you'll find everything in its place and exactly how you like it," she said. "In fact, I was just placing an order with one of the vendors. I noticed some of the table cloths needed replacing so I took the courtesy of ordering replacements." She leaned over then showed me a list of linens and other supplies that she had checked off. The name gracing the top of the invoice was for a company I had never heard of before.

"Thank you for taking the initiative," I said, staring at the list. "However, I have a preferred company that I use."

"Alabama linens and things," she said, nodding her head. "I saw their contact information saved in the vendor folder, but I thought we could do better. I found someone with far better prices and—"

"Price isn't an issue," I stopped her. "Alabama linens and supplies is locally owned and operated and I've been dealing with them since I started my business. We have a great business relationship and I'm pleased with them."

"I'm sure you are," she debated politely. "But sometimes

we have to step outside of our local area to save a few dollars. I know there is only like a three dollar difference, but think about how those dollars can add up over the years." Tabitha had a very good point with her debate; however, the problem was that the subject was not up for discussion. I didn't feel the need, nor did I have to explain to Tabitha that another reason why I continued to support ALT was because the company was minority female owned and I believed in supporting my sisters in business.

"Again, thank you for your initiative," I said pleasantly. "But I'm happy with our current supplier. You can cancel the order you made and I'll call my sales rep at ALT." Tabitha blinked several times while looking at me. I could see in her glare that she wanted to say something more, but she knew better.

"I'll take care of it," she said. "Is there anything else?" There was attitude in her voice and her stance. I wanted to tell her that right now was not her moment, and despite what I had been through I would still get in her ass. I chose to dismiss her behavior as stress and the fact that she needed a break.

"That's it for now," I said. She sucked on her teeth then turned on her heels and exited out the door. *No, the hell she didn't!* I thought. My conversation with Damon about promoting Tabitha resounded in my head. *Maybe he was right*, I thought to myself. I called my hubby to give him an update on how I was doing, and then I continued to go through the latest paperwork for the day. It took me just under an hour to catch up with my paperwork;

from there I tackled the mail.

As I sifted through the mail I found a card addressed to me with a return address from Selma, Alabama. It was from Betty Fletcher, Amel's mother. The card thanked me for the flowers I sent to her home and for the monetary donation. I had to fight back the tears as I read the handwritten expression of gratitude which included Ms. Fletcher stating she understood why I couldn't be in attendance at Amel's homegoing service. I had been so caught up in my own struggle that I had neglected to reach out to the woman concerning her loss; and naturally assumed my husband had.

When I placed the call to my husband to tell him thank you for being so thoughtful on my behalf, I discovered that he wasn't responsible; I then paged the hostess station and asked Kaitlyn to send Tabitha in to see me.

"Hey," Tabitha said, poking her head in the room.

"Did you send Ms. Fletcher flowers for Amel?" I asked.

"Yes. I thought that would be okay," she said frowning. "We took up a collection for her too. I apologize for signing your name. It won't happen again."

I still felt some kind of way about her behavior, but I also felt gratitude for Tabitha going above and beyond in this regard.

"Come in and sit down," I said. She shut the door then walked over and eased down in one of the chairs in front of my desk.

"That was really sweet of you," I said honestly. "Thank you."

"It was nothing," she said. "I know that's what you would have wanted and you would have done it for me."

I nodded my head in agreement. "I didn't mean to seem ungrateful," I said, staring at her.

"I didn't mean to step on your toes," she said, her voice cracking lightly. "I just wanted to prove to you and to myself that I could handle things in your absence. Please don't take my actions as disrespect because I didn't mean them that way."

The tension and mood between us slowly began to lighten.

"You did a great job," I reassured her.

"Thank you," she said. "So how are you feeling?"

"I'm better."

"One day at a time," she told me. She stood then adjusted her jacket. "Oh, I'll be back in uniform tomorrow."

"Don't worry about it," I said sincerely. "I'm okay with the way you're currently dressed."

Tabitha's eyes lit up with excitement. "Seriously?" She grinned.

"Yes, you look nice." I said. "In fact, I'm going to let Marilyn know that from here on out the lead hostess at the Ambiance 2 can now wear business casual attire there too." The glimmer in Tabitha's eyes darkened slightly, however, she continued to grin brightly.

"Sounds good," she said. "Well, let me get back to my job. Oh, the doctor is in the dining room and she asked about you."

Damon had mentioned that Shayla had come to visit while I was in recovery and that she was the one who had driven me to the hospital. The doctors told me at the time, that if I had been just a minute later in receiving treatment, it was possible that things would have been ten times worst. I knew that saving lives was a part of the pledge Shayla had taken as a physician, but I wanted to give her a personal thank you because she didn't have to help.

"Thanks Tabitha," I said as I stood up. "Can you make sure we cover her bill?"

"Sure can," Tabitha said, "she's in section E."

"Let her know I'll be out to see her in a moment," I instructed.

After Tabitha left, I went into my payroll database, calculated the total amount of Amel's final work hours and wrote a check in her mother's name with an additional amount added on. I stuffed the check in an envelope addressed to Mrs. Fletcher and placed the envelope in the bin for outgoing mail.

*****

"Hi there," I said, approaching the booth where Shayla sat. She was alone and looked completely engulfed in the book she held in front of her face.

"Octavia," she said cheerfully. She placed the book down and stood to greet me. She wore a fitted wrap dress that hugged her curves nicely. She gave me a friendly and unexpected hug before sitting back down. "Sit," she ordered. "How are you?"

"I'm better," I said, sliding in the booth opposite of her. "Thank you for asking and for the things you did. My husband told me you were the one that drove me to the ER."

"You don't remember?" she questioned.

"I remember bits and pieces," I said.

"You were going in and out," she said, shaking her head. "Sometimes experiencing extreme trauma can cause the mind to repress certain memories. It's not uncommon."

"Well, I've had my share of trauma in the last year," I said, thinking about my kidnapping. "Scratch that… the last four years!" I added remembering the day Beau attacked me and tried to kill Damon.

"I can relate," Shayla sighed. "I've seen my own."

"I can imagine," I said. "Being a doctor has got to be one of the hardest professions there is."

"It has its good moments," she said. "Like seeing someone, such as you make it through alright." She smiled at me then looked away. Her eyes and her expression became distant, like she was reliving a dark and troubling memory. "Then it has its low moments. The moments that come when you've done all you can do and it's still not enough. So you hope and pray, and pray and hope…only to finally realize it's too late." She paused for a moment before looking at me again. "I love my profession, but there is one thing I would trade it for it."

"What's that?"

"The ability to give life to the dead," she said sadly.

"There are times I wished *I* had that ability," I said truthfully. I dropped my eyes to the table not wanting her to see the tears that were attempting to surface. She reached across the table and stroked my arm gently.

"It's going to get better," she said gently.

"I'll be glad when it does," I said, looking up at her. "I really will."

"You know part of being in my line of work requires me to be a good listener," she said smiling. I appreciated her offer; but doctor or no doctor, I chose to reserve my thoughts and feelings to be shared with my family.

"Thank you, but I'm fine," I lied.

"I'm fine," Shayla recited. "Famous last words."

"I promise they won't be for me," I said. "Believe me."

"Here's the coffee you ordered," Tabitha said, coming up from behind us. "Octavia, I took the liberty of bringing you a cup too…both with a double shot of *Hershey's Chocolate Carmel* creamer."

"My favorite," Shayla said, waiting for Tabitha to sit the mugs down.

"Mine too," I said. "Thank you Tabitha."

"Not a problem," Tabitha said. "We'll have your entrée out in a minute." She left the table leaving Shayla and I sitting alone.

"So, what form of medicine do you practice?" I asked, taking a sip of my coffee. I figured the least I could do was make small talk.

"Neurology," she said.

"Do you work at Huntsville Hospital?"

"No, I have my own private practice," she said. "In the Hughes Road Plaza in Madison."

"And you drove to Huntsville for lunch?" I questioned. "You know we have a second location that's closer to your office."

"I know," she said, shrugging her shoulders. "I was in town shopping."

"A doctor who took the day off," I said. "I never knew there was such a thing."

Shayla laughed lightly. "There's not," she said. "I'm always on call, but I'm on vacation this week and one of my colleagues is filling in."

"Do you have plans to go anywhere?"

"I'm going to a conference in Montreal in a month," she said. "That will be vacation enough."

"I hear it's beautiful there," I told her.

"It is," she replied. "My husband...ex-husband as of last year...took me there for our one-year anniversary."

"How long were you married before you divorced?" I questioned.

"Eighteen years," she said, "We were together a total of twenty-two years. We were high school sweethearts."

I couldn't imagine putting eighteen years into my marriage only for it to fall apart. "Sorry to hear about that," I said. "Eighteen years of marriage is good in this day and age."

"Tell me about it," she laughed. "I have a few regrets, but for the most part we parted ways with fond and loving memories."

"That's a good thing," I said. "Do you ever talk or see each other?"

"No. Unfortunately not." She continued to sip her coffee while I sipped mine.

"How long have you and Damon been together?" Shayla asked.

"Four years," I said beaming proudly.

"Does the good outweigh the bad?" she asked. I paused only to consider all the joy Damon had brought into my life. It was true that the two of us had been through our share of pain and loss, but we had a plethora of beautiful memories to top it all off.

"Yes," I said. "It does."

"Then I wish you another fourteen years and then some," Shayla said sweetly.

"Thank you."

"So are you from Huntsville?" she asked.

"Yes," I answered. "And yourself?"

"I've been here for six years now," she said. "I'm originally from Chicago."

There was a silence between the two of us until she finally said, "I know how you feel."

"About what?" I asked curiously.

"I lost my own daughter a year ago." She paused, took a deep breath, then slowly exhaled. "She was killed by a drunk driver. She was only seventeen."

I listened quietly as Shayla described her daughter Halle to me. Her eyes lit up as she told me a story about a beautiful, vibrant young woman, who someday wanted to be a doctor and heal the world.

"She was my life," Shayla said. "After her death my marriage fell apart. Her father couldn't deal with it and I was of no help to him, I was suffering from my own depression. I finally learned to cope, but it was too late for my marriage."

"I'm sorry," I said sympathetically.

"Don't be," she said. "Our time was up. I understand that now…God had something greater in the plan." Shayla's optimism was inspiring. I could tell that there was still pain associated with her memories, but she refused to let them weigh her down. "So, if and when you're ready to talk…let me know." She reached inside the handbag sitting on the seat next to her and handed me a business card. "I'm always on call," she said, giving me a small smile.

"Thank you," I said with sincerity.

*****

After finishing my coffee, I left Shayla to enjoy her meal. I was feeling slightly woozy and the light tapping of an oncoming headache, which I was positive, was partially attributed to the fact that I had skipped breakfast. I decided to pick up a bottle of *Aleve* and then run to the bank for change. I would grab a bite to eat when I returned to the restaurant. I stepped out into the sunlight with my handbag in one hand and my keys in the other. The wind blew lightly, while a patch of tinted grey clouds began to form over head; an indication of rain on the horizon. As I walked down the sidewalk leading from the restaurant to the employee parking lot, an unsettling feeling began to come over me as chills etched down my spine. My palms began to sweat as my heart rate slowly increased.

"Thank you for everything Octavia." I heard a familiar voice say. I stopped then turned my head looking at the street. Amel stood in the middle of the street waving at me. *"Thank you for everything Octavia."* she repeated. I closed my eyes tightly, then opened them again; only to see the tan SUV slamming into her body, tossing her in the air. In my mind, the moment Amel was struck by the car was on constant repeat, and I couldn't get passed it nor press eject.

"No," I said, shaking my head. I stepped backwards, backing up against the side of the building. I felt the edges of the hard bricks against my back as the cryptic sounds of a woman screaming pierced the air around me.

"Thank you for everything Octavia...Thank you for everything ...For everything...For everything..." Amel's voice taunted me. My legs felt like cement as I walked from the side of the building, then ran; stumbling along the way to my car. I fumbled with my keys before finally pressing the open button on the starter.

"Thank you for everything Octavia...Thank you for everything...For everything...For everything...For everything..."

her voice continued to echo as I climbed into my car and slammed the door.

"Stop it!" I screamed, covering my ears. "Stop it!" I quickly jammed the key in the ignition, turned it to start, before turning the radio up as loud as it could go. I needed desperately to drown out the voice that was tormenting me; torturing me to no end. *I can still hear her!* I thought to myself. *Why can I still hear her?* I rocked back and forth in the driver's seat of my vehicle as tears streamed down my face. The voice that had been plaguing me slowly began to fade as the sounds of the bass coming from my stereo speakers began to shake me. My hand shook nervously as I reached out and decreased the volume on the radio. The music slowly faded, but the pounding continued; for it wasn't the bass coming from the speakers that I was now hearing, instead it was the beats of my heart.

"Boom. Boom. Boom. Boom. Boom. Boom."

The sound of my heart pounding, echoed loudly in my ears. I dabbed at my forehead with the back of my hand, soaking up the tiny droplets of perspiration that covered my brow. I sat in my car, frozen in place, with my hands gripping the leather steering wheel tightly.

What's happening to me? I asked myself. I had an unsettling feeling that I was being watched; a rush of paranoia fell over me and I began to feel that something terrible was lurking outside my car. My mouth felt like it was losing all moisture and became incredibly dry. I inhaled through my nose attempting to calm my distressed nerves and racing heart, but my airway felt like it was getting smaller with every second; like there was a vacuum in my lungs sucking out my breath. I leaned forward resting my head against the steering wheel.

Breathe Octavia, I recited to myself. *Breathe.*

It wasn't working. There was a knock on the car window that sent me scrambling over the gear shift and against the passenger's side door. Tabitha stood by the driver's side window; staring at me.

"Are you okay?" she asked. I shook my head no as my tears combined with my sweat and stung my eyes.

She grabbed the door handle in an attempt to open the door. "Octavia it's locked," she said. "Unlock the door."

I wanted to honor her request, but I was frozen in place. I was trapped, a prisoner in my own head, shackled by my own thoughts.

"Octavia," she pleaded. "Please open the door!"

My struggle to breath continued as I pulled my knees up to my chest.

"I'll be back!" Tabitha yelled, turning and then ultimately running towards the building. I placed my head in between my knees, trying desperately to calm my breathing.

"Octavia!" I slowly raised my head and saw Shayla standing next to Tabitha outside the window. "Octavia, it's okay," Shayla said. "Everything is fine…take a deep breath for me."

I shook my head. I was trying, but my lungs wouldn't allow it. *I can't,* I thought. *I can't!*

"Yes, you can," Shayla stated as if she was reading my mind. "Yes, you can. Focus on your breathing...nothing else. Close your eyes Octavia."

I closed my eyes.

"Focus only on the darkness and your breath. Feel the air filling your lungs and pushing through your airway."

I did as Shayla ordered. I took a deep-cleansing breath, inhaling through my nostrils and finally exhaling through my parted lips. I repeated the steps until my heart rate slowly began to decrease. *Thank you God,* I thought.

"Octavia open the door," Shayla ordered. "Open the door."

My body continued to shake as I slowly turned in the seat then unlocked the car door.

Chapter 8

Damon

"Octavia!" I called, walking through the foyer of our home. "Babe!" I stepped up the staircase, taking the stairs two at a time as thoughts of worry and concern plagued my mind. Tabitha called me to let me know Octavia had an anxiety attack and that she was driving her home. I immediately left my office without a second thought. I knew I should have put up more of a fight when Octavia insisted she was okay. It was my responsibility to put my foot down; and now, just as I feared, something happened.

"Octavia!" I called from the top of the stairs. I rushed down the hall taking my jacket off as I approached our room.

"I'm in here," she called from the bedroom. I entered the room tossing my jacket on the dresser. Octavia lay barefoot on top of the comforter curled up clutching a pillow to her chest.

"Baby," I said, rushing to the side of the bed.

"I'm okay," she whispered. I eased down, sitting on the edge of the bed.

"Tabitha called me," I told her.

"I don't know what happened," she mumbled. "I was fine, but then I came out...I was leaving to go to the bank and I could hear her."

"Hear who?" I asked, rubbing her back.

"Amel," she said. "Her voice just kept calling out to me and then I kept visualizing her getting struck by that car..."

I listened carefully as Octavia gave me the details that led to her panic attack. Her voice was on a childlike tone that alarmed me. I brushed it off, assuming she was still on edge from her attack.

"Once my breathing slowed, I opened the door," she continued. "I was too embarrassed to go back into the restaurant, so Tabitha volunteered to bring me home; but to keep the other employees from knowing something was wrong, I just drove myself home instead."

"You have nothing to be embarrassed about," I reassured her. "You lived through more than most have ever seen. That's a lot to deal with boo."

"Clearly I'm not dealing," she said, pulling herself up on the bed. She reclined against the headboard and looked at me. "I can't believe I went off like that."

"You're being too hard on yourself," I said. "Maybe it's just too soon to return to work and the reminder of what took place there."

"Or maybe I'm just too weak to handle it," she debated.

"You are a lot of things," I said cutting her off. "But weak isn't one of them."

"That's how I felt," she said looking away. "Weak and lost. I couldn't get it together..."

I couldn't change the way Octavia was feeling, but I wanted, no, I needed her to believe that everything was going to be okay.

"We are going to get through this," I promised. "Together. No matter what it takes." She wrapped her arms around my neck, pressing her breast against my chest.

"I love you Damon," she whispered. I secured my arms tightly around her waist, holding her tightly.

"I love you more," I said, pressing my lips against her neck.

"Maybe what I need is a nice hot bath," she said, pulling away. She ran her fingers through her hair then exhaled softy. "Maybe it'll help clear my head."

"I'm on it," I said. I helped her remove her clothes until she was wearing nothing but her beautiful brown skin. I scanned my eyes over her naked body, admiring the cut and lift of her full breasts, the tightness of her chocolate nipples, the small pudge she still carried around her stomach, and the faint discolored stretch marks that now graced her hips. Even with the extra pounds she gained while carrying our son, my wife was one of the sexiest women I had ever seen.

I tucked her underneath the covers to allow me time to run her bath water. I lit Octavia's favorite vanilla scented candles then placed them around the Jacuzzi tub in our master bathroom. I wanted my wife to unwind and relax her body and I was hoping that she would be able to ease her troubled mind.

"You are too good to me," she sighed, while I assisted her into the tub.

"Not good enough," I commented. She settled in the bubble-filled water then reclined.

"I owe you dinner," she said.

"I have dinner under control," I said, standing next to the bathtub. "We can order in. Your choice."

"I can call Grille 29 and order us something," she suggested, stroking her arms. "You can pick it up when you go get Jazz from daycare."

"I was planning to ask Charles to pick her up," I advised her. Octavia's eyes grew wide. It was my desire to have my father in law pick up Jasmine because I didn't want to leave Octavia alone; not even for a second.

"Please don't," she begged. "Mama will know something is wrong. I don't want to worry her. She is doing so well right now, and I've worried her enough. Please Damon, let's just keep this between the two of us."

Charlene was so resilient that at times I forgot that it was not too long ago that she had battled with cancer. The cancer was now in remission and she seemed stronger than ever, but I knew part of maintaining her health was also dependent upon keeping her stress at a minimum. I bent down to my knees by the edge of the tub. I observed the look in my love's eyes while pondering her request. She looked a hundred percent better than she had when I first arrived home.

"Okay," I finally agreed.

*****

I picked up my daughter from daycare then drove to Grille 29 to pick up the order Octavia called in for the three of us. The savory aroma rising from the styrofoam carry-out plates I carried in the bag in my hand made my stomach grumble, to the point that it felt like it was going to beat a path through my back. I had no clue what Octavia ordered for the two of us, but whatever it was, it smelled good as hell and I was anxiously awaiting digging into it. I held my daughter's hand with one hand while carrying the bag in the other as Jasmine and I walked toward the front door of the restaurant. We were almost at the exit when a familiar face stepped inside the restaurant door. I smiled while observing the tall woman with brown skin and sepia-colored eyes.

"Tamara?" I said, stopping.

"D!" she cheered. "How are you?" I dropped Jasmine's hand just long enough to hug Savoy's sister, then I took my daughter's hand again. Tamara was a year older than Savoy and one of four girls in the Breedwell family.

"I'm good," I said. "How are you?"

"I'm okay," she said. Her full cheeks spread as her lips formed a smiled. "Hey little mama!" Jasmine looked from

Tamara to me then to Tamara again but never replied. I didn't know if that was due to the continuous lessons from her parents that said, "Do not talk to strangers" or if she was going to have an instant dislike of the Breedwell women much like her mother.

Octavia's distaste for Tamara, her mother, and her sisters was solely based of the way they reacted when Savoy chose to marry Shontay. When it came to her best friend, Octavia had a strict policy of loyalty and there was no questioning nor going around it. It was simple, if you didn't love Shontay, you didn't love Octavia.

"It's okay," Tamara said, through clenched teeth. "I can see the apple didn't fall far from the tree. She is just like her mother," she said nicely. "And just as beautiful."

"She is," I agreed. "And I'm sure both will come around someday." I wasn't willing to put money on that, but I was still encouraging Tamara to remain optimistic.

"So, what are you doing here?" I asked.

"I live here now."

"What? Since when?"

"Yep, I've been here for a little over three weeks now," she said.

"So you and Stan finally decided to leave Georgia?" Stan was Tamara's husband. The two of them had been married for several years and operated an interior design company together. I'd been around Stan a couple of times and from what I could gather, he seemed like a decent man and Savoy never spoke against him.

"No, me. Not me and Stan," she said. "I made the

decision..alot of things have changed in the last year."

I could tell there was a lot more Tamara wanted to share with me, but Jasmine, who was now tugging on my hand, reminded me that it was time for us to go.

"Tamara, I have got to get this food home," I said quickly. "Do you still have my number?"

"I think so," she said. I reached into my back pocket and pulled out one of my business cards and handed it to her.

"It was good seeing you," she said. "I'll give you call."

"Take care." I told her before leaving the restaurant.

Chapter 9

Octavia

The next day it took every breath in my body to convince Damon that I was okay and that I would be perfectly fine at home alone; but I'm sure it took more out of him to convince me to stay at home. I felt my panic attack was nothing more than a fluke; a consequence of not properly eating and just being mentally exhausted. Damon felt I needed more time to recuperate from the physical trauma I had been through. I decided not to argue with him and to grant his wish of taking it easy for a little while longer. Tabitha seemed perfectly fine working double shifts, and despite or minor run in, I knew she was a good and hardworking employee.

I had to pledge, and damn near give a sample of blood to get Damon out the house. Don't get me wrong, I loved the way my hubby insisted upon being there for me, but I was craving some me time. I needed to process my thoughts and attempt to get a grip on my emotions without his constant desire to smother me with attention.

I sat curled up on the sofa in my family room scanning over the pages of the latest edition of *Ebony* magazine, when my home phone let off the distinctive ring indicating someone was at our gated entrance. I made my way to the kitchen to observe the monitors connected to our security system and I saw a skinny Caucasian male standing outside of a black delivery van. The van had the words, "Cowan's Flowers" printed in bright pink lettering on the side.

Damon, I thought to myself.

"Hello," I answered.

"I have a delivery for Mrs. Whitmore," the man said.

"I'll let you through," I said.

Five minutes later I smiled brightly while looking at the bouquet of yellow roses and the gift basket that the man brought to my door. The flowers and the basket were from my employees. I sat the glass vase that contained the dozen long-stemmed roses on the console table against my foyer wall, then carried the large basket into the kitchen. I stood at my kitchen island ripping open the clear plastic cellophane like a child on Christmas morning. Granted, I've received gifts and little tokens of love on a regular basis from Damon, but I always got excited from any gift I received. The last gift I was given from someone outside of my husband was when Damon's now deceased half-brother, Kelly, gave me the tiny angel that sits on the corner of my desk at the Ambiance. The handcrafted angel was created in the image of my daughter. Even after Kelly's death and his participation in Gator's plot to kill my husband, I still couldn't bring myself to get rid of the little porcelain token. It wasn't because of Kelly or any unresolved feelings, but more so because it was truly a thoughtful gift despite the intentions of the man behind it.

Inside the basket was a plain handwritten note with Tabitha's signature. The message was simple but sweet: "Relax and feel better soon." Inside there was a variety of herbal tea leaves, including my favorite; green-mango peach. There was also fresh honey, shortbread cookies, and a pretty pink china teacup and matching saucer. I smiled from the thoughtfulness of my employee as I picked up my cordless phone and dialed Tabitha's number.

"Hey Octavia," she answered happily. "How are you?"

"I'm well," I said. I balanced the phone on my shoulder while preparing the water to steep my tea. "I just got your gift. Thank you, that was really sweet of you."

"No problem," she said. "It's my pleasure. Every one chipped in. Kaitlyn put the basket together."

"Well, tell everyone I said thank you for me." I said. "Let Kaitlyn know she did a great job with the basket."

"I certainly will," she said. "Make sure you enjoy and relax!"

"I will. I'm in the process of making me a cup of the green-peach mango now," I advised her. "And the good thing is, I will have it all to myself. Damon hates any and all forms of green tea." I laughed lightly.

"I remember," Tabitha said, from the other end of the phone. "You told me."

I hadn't realized how many little details about myself and my family I had shared with Tabitha over the years. It was clear there had been several and she had been paying attention.

"You know more about me than I realized," I said.

"When you have someone you look up to or you consider family, you pay attention," Tabitha said. "To me it's kinda how you tell them thank you and let them know you appreciate them."

There was a sound in her voice that I couldn't quite put my finger on. I could hear her admiration, but there was something more there; something that I had clearly been missing.

"I can understand that," I said, sincerely.

"Can you?"

"Yes, I really can," I stated.

"Good," she said firmly. "Well boss, you know I love you, but duty calls."

"Get back to work," I said smiling. "Call me if you need me and thank you again."

"I got it," she said, confidently "Talk to you later."

I finished preparing my tea, grabbed my magazine and headed out to my patio to enjoy the sunshine. I settled in against one of the two matching chaise lounges Damon and I had sitting by our pool; then reclined, stretching my legs out in front of me. The smooth, tangy, tart taste of my beverage warmed my throat as I sipped slowly from my cup.

I admired the view of the vibrant green grass that made up my lawn as memories of the day Damon and I took our first set of vows, carried me down the beautiful streets of "memory lane." I could see the small crowd of family and friends watching with smiles of joy planted on their faces. The harmonious sounds of the six-piece orchestra playing as Damon stood waiting for me; looking like nothing less than a king. I took another sip from the cup as my own smile grew from anticipation. Looking down over my body, I could see the spaghetti-strapped *Vera Wang* gown my mother-in-law purchased for me. I could feel my baby bump and the light flutters of my then unborn daughter Jasmine, moving and kicking inside of me.

"Are you ready?" Daddy asked, smiling at me. He stood beside me wearing a dark, designer tuxedo. His honey-brown eyes shining brightly as he looked at me.

"As ready as I'll ever be," I said. I stood allowing the hem and train of my gown to fall freely around my ankles, covering the designer shoes Ilene had purchased for me. I reached for my father's arm then realized he was no longer there; instead there was Beau. He stood smiling at me, wearing sagging jeans with a matching denim shirt, and wheat colored *Timberlands*. His dark skin was smooth and flawless, but his eyes were clouded and glazed by the faint color of red. He ran his hands over his neat corn rows while holding a tightly rolled blunt in between his fingers. He raised the lit El to his lips then took a long drag before blowing smoke out his mouth.

"What's up Ma?" He asked, gazing at me.

"No," I said, taking a step back. I closed my eyes wishing the vision before me would go away. "It's not real. It's not real." I repeated aloud. I opened my eyes and he was gone along with my gown, wedding guests, Damon, and the orchestra. I ran my fingers through my hair, trying to make sense of what was happening, reminding myself of where I was.

"Sis!" I heard the sweet voice I missed so much, calling me.

"Shontay?" I asked, scanning my eyes from one corner of the property to the other.

"In here Octavia…" she called out to me. I zoomed in on the guesthouse. The heart-warming sound of my best friend's laugh was enticing me.

"Shontay," I said, walking around the pool towards the guest house.

"In here Tavia," she sung. I stepped along the grass, walking quickly in the direction of Shontay's voice. I stepped up onto the landing of the guesthouse as Shontay's voice continued to call me.

"In here sis," she said. My heart began to race as I turned the handle to the guesthouse then slowly pushed open the door. Shontay stood in the middle of the room, wearing fitted jeans and the purple off the shoulder sweater that I had given her nearly eight years before for her birthday. Her hair was blown out in a full afro, reminiscent of the style Pam Greer wore in for the role of *Foxy Brown*. She smiled at me, then shook her head.

"Tay?" I asked. There was something in the dark crevices of my mind reminding me that what I was seeing wasn't real. That my friend, whom I called my sister, could not be standing before me, because I had witnessed her in her final moments of life. I had watched as she crossed the bridge of life into the dreaded waters of death. However, the love and the longing inside of me that needed one more day, one more hour, minute, or even second with her wanted what I thought I was seeing to be true. Shontay opened her arms wide, inviting me to embrace her. I moved quickly to where she stood as tears trickled like water from a leaky faucet down my face."

"I missed you…" I said softly, "so much…" I reached for her, but captured nothing but air. "Noo!" I cried, looking around the room frantically. She was gone. "Shontay! Shontay!" I cried. My voice echoed in my ears as I scanned the room with my eyes. I dropped to the floor, allowing my sorrow to overflow through my tears. The sounds of my cries echoed, resounding like the clashing of snare drums. I stayed on the floor kneeling like a sinner before a Holy alter, seeking redemption and relief from the thoughts plaguing me. The sounds of my sobs slowly began to dissipate as moans of pleasure and ecstasy filled the air around me. I raised my head while slowly rising to my feet. The moans were mine, and they were coming from the bed. I lay spread eagle across the silky comforter with someone kneeling in between my open legs. I slowly pulled my feet in closer to the X-rated scene my imagination had brought before me. I knew all too well of the chocolate complexioned man who held my thighs in his clutches and his face buried in between my lower lips. It was Kelly.

"*Mmm...yessss...yessss!*"

"Stop it!" I yelled at myself. "Stop it now!"

I ran out the door of the guesthouse, tracking quickly through the grass to my home. I slammed the French doors shut behind me, then locked the door. My skin felt oily and rigid from the sweat and goose bumps that hovered over my skin. The sounds of Beau's, Shontay's and Kelly's voices comingled in the space around me. They were pushing me closer and closer to the edge of madness, and I couldn't bear to hear them any longer. I paced back and forth across the kitchen floor as the voices began to fade. The soft sounds of a baby crying caused me stop my pacing. The child's lungs were strong and the cry was like a siren indicating danger.

Thoughts of guilt and shame played in my head from my lack of concern when I viewed my deceased son. I felt a wave rising inside of me with every second. I struggled to hold on to my inner peace in an attempt to salvage a portion of my sanity. However, the tragic memories of the child I lost pounded over and over again inside my head—bouncing from wall to wall— causing it to ache unbearably. I needed instant relief, the kind that no amount of Ibuprofen or aspirin could provide, and I needed it now. I was tired of loss after loss. Sick of death. So, I let go; allowing the destructive emotional tide of pain and sorrow to carry me out to the icy, dark sea of grief.

I marched to my kitchen cabinet where Damon and I stored our spirits; retrieving an un-open bottle of *Rosa*. I sat the bottle on the counter, then dug deeper inside the cabinet until I found a bottle of *Ciroc*. I quickly opened the bottle, wasting no time on getting a glass and turned the bottle up to my lips, allowing the liquid to burn the inside of my chest. I took another shot, followed by another, and one more until I heard the cries no more.

I walked out the kitchen through the foyer of my home and finally up the stairs leading to my bedroom. I stop my strides and stood, gripping my pain reliever in one hand, staring at the closed door leading to what should have been my son's nursery. I opened the door, observing the bright yellow décor. I took another shot, this time feeling nothing but disgust and anguish. The room was too bright; brightness represented happiness and joy. There was nothing joyous about the things surrounding me. I took another gulp from the bottle then hurried back downstairs and out the door to our detached garage. I dug through Damon's tool box and pulled items from the shelves that I knew could complete the job I felt awaited me inside the nursery.

G STREET CHRONICLES
A NEW URBAN DYNASTY

WWW.GSTREETCHRONICLES.COM

Chapter 10

Damon

I dialed my home phone number again and got the same result I had been receiving for the last thirty minutes. The phone rang and rang until the voicemail picked up. I had already tried Octavia's cellphone several times, but much like when I called our landline, I got her voicemail.

Maybe she's sleeping, I thought to myself.

I had spoken with my wife earlier in the day, but I once again wanted to be sure she was still feeing alright. When I was unable to reach her again, I decided to check with Charles and Charlene. I called my in-laws making light conversation while nonchalantly checking to see if they had spoken to their daughter. I knew instantly from their questions that they had not. I ended the conversation with them, then stood, preparing to leave my office and go home, when Louisa buzzed me to let me know I had a visitor. A moment later, Tamara walked through my office door. She wore a fitted above the knee wrapped dress. I had forgotten all about the text she had sent me that morning asking if the two of us could sit down for a meeting. Naturally my focus and thoughts had been on my family.

"Did I catch you at a bad time?" she asked, observing my expression.

"Um, no," I lied. "I was just going to make a quick run." I could see the instant disappointment in her face.

"I can come back," she said. I contemplated her offer, then decided maybe it was best if I didn't rush home. I was worried about my wife, but at the same time I didn't want to antagonize her further. I decided to keep the commitment I made to Tamara.

"No need," I said. "It can wait. Please sit down." I resumed my position back behind my desk as Tamara sat down in the chair on the other side. "So, what's up?"

"I need a job or hobby," she said bluntly. "Something to keep me busy." I remembered when Jasmine and I bumped into Tamara at Grille 29 that she stated a lot of things had changed with her in the past year, but I didn't remember her stating that closing her business was one of them.

"What happened to your interior design company?" I asked curiously.

"The interior design company belongs to Stan," she said.

"Your husband," I said with raised eyebrows.

"My soon to be ex-husband," she enlightened me.

"I'm sorry to hear that," I said sincerely.

"Don't be," Tamara said. "Things have been bad for a while now. I just finally got tired of fighting a losing battle and decided enough was enough." She looked at me then frowned. "Besides, life is too short to be unhappy. I think we both know that." I knew she was referring to her brother.

"I agree," I said.

"So, that's why I'm here," she said. "I figured a new city and a new start."

"How are you financially?" I asked.

"Financially, I'm good," she smiled. "Savoy made sure of that. He left enough money for me, mama, and my sisters to eat and eat well. My desire to work is just that...a desire."

"So why not launch your own business here?" I questioned. "The city is growing with every passing moment. Now would be an excellent time for a start up."

Tamara looked like she was considering my suggestion. "I'm not sure if here is where I want to be permanently," she said, crossing her legs. "Don't get me wrong, I'm digging it so far, but you never know where the winds of chance may blow."

I knew what Tamara meant, but wasn't saying, was that she didn't want to get too comfortable because despite what she stated about her marriage to Stan, she was still open to the possibility of the two of them getting back together.

"Right now I have a full staff," I advised her.

"D, I'm family," she said. "There's always room for family."

"Not for family who knows nothing about investment or money management," I said, shaking my head. "I have not forgotten that at one point in time your piggy bank was overdrawn." I laughed while remembering the stories Savoy told me about Tamara's poor money management skills. It wasn't that she didn't have the money to cover her bills, she just chose not to pay them and when she did it was after she had tons of fees and penalties.

"You got jokes," she said sarcastically. "That was many moons ago. I haven't bounced a check in like eight months." She smacked her lips. "Maybe nine." I stared at her in disbelief.

"There is no way in hell I'm letting you near my clients or their money," I said relaxing in my chair.

"I'm playing D!" she laughed. "I've been on my shit for real."

"I'm not falling for it," I said. "In fact the two of us should sit down and look at how you're managing. Seriously."

"Okay," she giggled. "You sound just like Savoy."

"He knew!"

"I'm not admitting that," she said. "But I will say I've heard more than twice that I could use a class or two in finance."

"Hmm..humm," I said. "You've heard it because it's true."

"Whatever, "she said. "Just pencil me in for your next appointment. I'll be ready."

I wrapped up my meeting with Tamara, agreeing to meet with her the next day. She inquired about the three of us, meaning me, her, and Octavia getting together for dinner. I told her I would mention it, but I knew the chances were slim to none of that happening. Last night when I told Octavia I bumped into Tamara, she was fine with me keeping in touch with her. She understood the family connection and that Savoy would have done the same for me, but she was quite clear that she had no interest in being friends with Tamara or any of her sisters.

I walked Tamara out, then continued with the paperwork I had put on hold while trying to contact Octavia. An hour later, I was interrupted by Louisa paging me through the speaker on my phone.

"Damon the daycare is on line one," Louisa announced.

"Thank you," I said. "This is Damon." I answered the call waiting for me.

"Mr. Whitmore, it's Sherry the director at Providence Day Care."

"Hi Sherry, what can I do for you?" I asked, curious as to why the woman was calling me.

"I was calling to see who was planning to pick up Jasmine."

"My wife," I stated, looking at my watch. It was already 5:30 p.m. Octavia and I never picked up Jasmine later than 4:30 p.m. and we never picked up our daughter after the schools 5:00 p.m. closing time.

"I tried calling Mrs. Whitmore, but I was unable to reach her," Sherry informed me.

"I apologize," I said, rising from my chair. "I'll be there in fifteen minutes."

*****

"Wait here," I ordered Jasmine who was sitting on the sofa in our family room. I walked through the kitchen making sure the doors leading outside to our pool were not only locked, but secured with the child safety latch before running upstairs to look for Octavia. The scent of fresh paint greeted me as soon as I stepped into the hallway. "What the hell," I mumbled, as I came to the nursery room door. The bedroom door was covered in red paint; from the hinges to the door handle itself. I knew the door was a sign that what was waiting for me on the other side wasn't good; but nothing could have prepared me for the scene before me. There were splatters of red paint on the carpet and dripping from the drapes and blinds. The entire room had been splashed in bright red paint, including the crib, changing table, and even the window.

"Octavia," I called, rushing into our bedroom. The room was empty. I instantly began to panic. I entered the bathroom and found her sprawled out on the floor. She was snoring loudly and lying next to a half empty bottle of liquor with splashes of paint on her clothes, arms and hands. It took me almost two and a half hours to get Octavia cleaned up and get the paint off her skin. I was sure the task would have been ten times easier if I didn't have to pause in between the task to hold her over the toilet while she vomited. Six hours later, I sat alone in the home theater in shorts and a t-shirt, staring at the television with the volume so low the sounds were almost inaudible.

"Where's Jazz?"

I turned around at the sound of Octavia's voice. She stood in the doorway wearing the gown I slipped on her after giving her a bath. Her hair was disheveled and her eyes were bloodshot red.

"She's spending the night with Charles and Charlene," I said. I hit the power button on the remote, turning off the TV.

"You called them?"

"Yes," I said. "I thought it was best."

"For whom?" she asked, folding her arms across her chest. "You or me?"

"For everyone," I said calmly. I knew part of Octavia's attitude was attributed to the fact that she was still somewhat drunk. I chose to take that fact into consideration when responding to her.

"So, you make decisions however you want and fuck what I have to say," she snapped. "I really wish you would learn to respect my wishes! You don't listen...you never fucking listen!"

"I come home and one of our bedrooms looks like Jasmine had a paint party," I said while standing to my feet. "Then I find you passed out drunk to the point that you barely understand your own name!"

"You told me to relax," she said sarcastically.

"I told you to relax," I said staring at her. "Relax. Why don't you tell me how you got, 'get pissy ass drunk to the point that you forget to pick our daughter up from daycare' out of the word, relax? Hum? Tell me how that happened?" *Silence.* "But you say I don't fucking listen? You might want to check the mirror boo." She looked at me with tears in her eyes then turned and walked out the room. "Damnit!" I huffed. I had let my temper get the best of me and that was the last thing I ever wanted to do with Octavia. I instantly felt bad and the desire to smooth things over with her. "Octavia," I called after her. I exited the theater following behind her. She ran inside our bedroom and slammed the door closed behind her. "Octavia, I'm sorry," I said bagging on the door. My apologies were in vain. The door was locked and she refused to open it.

Chapter 11

Octavia

I felt like crap twice laid the next morning. My feelings were not only from my hangover, but from the realization that I had been so caught up in my madness that I forgot about my daughter. I made myself a promise that it would never happen again, and I was determined, come hell or high water, that I would keep my promise. I came downstairs and found Damon sprawled out across the sofa wearing basketball shorts and a t-shirt. The sight of him reminded me of when I woke up in the hospital and he was sleeping in the chair next to the bed. I knew I was wrong for how I had spoken to him, and he was justified for his response, but that didn't prevent me from being angry. Sometimes the truth is the most flammable fuel for a fire. The house phone rang as I entered the kitchen, I frowned instantly when I saw my mother's name on the caller ID.

"Good morning mommy," I said politely.

"Why didn't you tell me about the attack?" Mama immediately asked.

"I didn't want to worry you," I said, honestly.

"So your passing out drunk after redecorating in abstract wouldn't worry me?" She said with sarcasm dripping in her voice.

I pulled the refrigerator door open and removed eggs and vegetables for an omelet. I slammed the door as Damon came dragging into the kitchen. He maneuvered around me, opened the refrigerator and removed a bottle of apple juice before sitting down at the kitchen table.

"You weren't supposed to know about that," I said, rolling my eyes at him. "I guess honor has taken on a whole new meaning." Damon looked at me with raised eyebrows then exhaled.

"Don't you dare blame Damon," Mama ordered. "He was right to call us and he was right to want to take care of you."

"Why did that require you coming to pick up Jasmine?" I asked, placing a skillet on top of the stove.

"Did you really want your daughter to see you in that condition?"

Mama had a point. I didn't want my daughter to see me inebriated. It was a bad look no matter how young she was.

"No," I answered.

"Alright then, stop being hard on the man who loves you enough to realize that."

"Fine," I said.

"I love you baby you know this ," Mama said gently.

"I love you too."

"But I think you may want to talk to someone," she continued. "Get some therapy."

"I'm fine Mama," I said. "I just need a little time." There was no way I was going to see a therapist. I didn't need some over-educated , over-achiever telling me what I already feared inside; that I was losing my mind. Hell, that part I understood!

"Octavia, you have to talk about what's happened," she said. "It's not good to keep your emotions bottled up."

"I'm not Mama," I said, attempting to convince her. "Just give me a little more time and if I don't sort things out, I'll follow your suggestion. I promise." Mama took a deep breath then exhaled.

"Okay pumpkin," she said. "Hold on your father would like to speak with you."

I listened as my Dad gave me a lecture almost identical to the one Mama had given me. When he was finished I told him I loved him and to kiss Jasmine for me. I hung up the phone then redirected my attention to the breakfast I was preparing. I could feel Damon watching me out the corner of my eye. His gawking was pissing me off with every second.

"Do you want an omelet?" I asked, looking him directly in the eyes.

"Yes please," he answered.

I picked up one of the eggs then slammed it against

the side of the skillet, causing pieces of the shell to fall inside. I disregarded the shells then dumped the egg in the skillet tossing the remaining shell on the kitchen counter. I didn't wait for the egg to start cooking before I threw the veggies on top.

"I can't believe you broke your promise," I ranted, staring at Damon. "You told them about what happened at the Ambiance."

"Octavia they needed to know," he said. "And what was I supposed to do? You won't talk to me."

"I'm talking to you now!"

"No, you're yelling at me now," he corrected me. "And you're avoiding the problem."

"Oh, I know what the problem is," I said, angry. I turned the stove off then removed the skillet. I snatched a plate down from the cabinet overhead then I dumped the partially cooked omelet on the plate. I carried the plate over to the table and dropped the concoction in front of Damon. "The problem is everyone wants to fix me," I continued. "I don't need fixing!"

"You need time," he said, completing my thought. "But if I remember correctly, before when I said you needed time—you said you were fine." I was once again bothered by the truth that flowed from my husband's lips. I remained silent while watching. He stared from the plate to me then back to the plate again.

"I think I'll just have cereal," he said.

"Fix it yourself," I said, stomping off.

"Don't worry," he said. "I was planning on it."

Chapter 12

Damon

"You call this a filing system?" I stared at the three shoe boxes of receipts and bills sitting on my desk in front of me, waiting on Tamara's response.

"It works for me," she said.

"You know you're wrong for this," I said.

"Don't knock the method," she laughed. "I have it color coded. If it's in the red shoe box it's business related. The brown is personal."

"And the white one?" I asked.

"The white one is a variety box…you never know what you might find." She smiled innocently.

"Do you think we can find a budget and a check book in it?" I asked, lifting the top of the box.

"Budget? What budget…Checkbook…*maybe*."

"This is going to take more than a couple of hours,"

I told her.

"I got plenty of time," she said, clasping her hands together. "I'll even buy you lunch."

"Are you sure you can afford it?" I teased. "Look at your filing system."

"Ha…ha," she said, rolling her eyes. "Of course I can. I robbed my piggybank."

"Let me just double check my schedule," I told her. I logged on to my laptop and saw that I had no important meetings or anything on my agenda besides sending my wife flowers. I picked up the phone and asked Louisa if she could handle the task for me.

"How many dozens?"

"Two," I said. I thought about the runny, shell-filled omelet Octavia had made for me earlier that morning. "On second thought Ms. Louisa, let's make it three."

"I gotcha boss," Louisa advised me.

"Thank you." I looked up and Tamara was staring at me smiling.

"What?"

"You and my brother," she chuckled. "You believe in spoiling your women."

"I believe, much like your brother believed, that when you have a good thing you show your appreciation."

"Your women would never make it with an ordinary man," Tamara commented. "You get flowers on holidays and when he knows he messed up and he's trying to get his ass out the doghouse."

We both laughed.

"Wait a minute...what do you mean by 'ordinary man?'" I asked, leaning forward in my chair. "I'm an ordinary man. I put my pants on one leg at a time just like the next man; and any man that values what he has is willing to take care of that which he's been given. There's nothing extraordinary about that...it's just real."

"I feel that," she said. "But sometimes it's the extent of how you do it that sets you a part from the rest. That extra little something like, nawh, don't send her one dozen let's make it three." She cocked her head to the side while smirking at me. "That's what makes you extraordinary."

"Thank you for that," I said.

"Savoy was the same way," Tamara said, softly. "He would break his neck to prove his love."

"The definition of a good man," I said.

"A walking, breathing, example of a good one," Tamara said solemnly. "We need more like him in the world... more like you." She had a look of sincere appreciation on her face. An expression of respect that could only come from some who truly knows and understands you. The two of us sat in silence, staring at each other.

"So, you ready to get this party started," I finally said, opening the boxes.

"Let's do it," she said.

I stood removing my suit jacket and hung it over the back of my chair.

"Wait till you get my bill," I joked. "You'll see just how extraordinary I am. Bringing shoeboxes up in here like you going to Pooky's backdoor tax services…what's wrong with you woman?"

The two of us laughed again. In that moment of camaraderie I was temporarily taken from my own problems and put in a place of refreshing peace.

*****

I decided to have Bento Box, a local Asian restaurant, cater lunch for the entire office. It had been a while since I surprised my team, and I figured there was no time like the present. Tamara and I sat at the small conference table inside my office enjoying our meals and reminiscing on the past.

"You remember that hoodrat you and Savoy use to date?" Tamara asked. "What was her name?"

"Taliyah," I answered.

"Taliyah," Tamara chuckled, shaking her head. "That's how the two of you met; right?"

"Yes."

"Whew! She had yours and my brother's nose wide open."

"I was fond of her," I said, stroking the hairs on my chin. "I'll admit that, but my nose was far from open."

"Whatever! She had both of ya'll running your little asses over there feeding her and breaking her off bread. That hoe was a pimp."

"She had us twisted," I said, thinking back. "But it was all good in the end." I smiled to myself thinking about how Savoy and I had ended the night we found out about one another on one of the best notes two straight men could ever share with one woman.

"Oh, and I know ya'll ran the train on her," Tamara said, busting me. "You know me and my brother were thicker than thieves back in the day." I had been denying the truth about the train since I had left that fact out when telling Octavia about how me and Savoy met. I was unusually surprised to hear it, but not shocked that Savoy had spilled the news to Tamara.

"We did not!" I said, pretending to be offended.

"A lie don't care who tells it," Tamara giggled. "Don't worry, he spared me from all the nasty little details, but he said it went down!" She raised her hands in the air then lowered them simultaneously. I erupted in laughter.

"You know if you mention this to any one I will deny it to the grave," I warned.

"Your secret's safe," she said.

"I can't believe he told you that," I said.

"We were cool like that," she said. "He was your best friend and mine too. At least he was until he met..."

"Shontay," I concluded.

"Yep," Tamara said seriously. She moved her fork across the plastic plate in front of her, pushing her food from one side to the other.

"Is that the reason you disliked her?" I asked.

"Part of it," she confessed. "I know it was stupid and childish, but you have to keep in mind Savoy was the backbone of our family after my father passed. Then he comes here and falls for a *married* woman. The next thing we know, he's chasing her all around the globe…we just felt he could have gotten, and deserved better."

I understood where Tamara and the rest of the Breedwell women were coming from, but the decision wasn't theirs to make on how or whom Savoy chose to love.

"Shontay was a wonderful woman," I said. "She was loving and kind hearted. I'm not saying that the way their relationship developed was right, but I am saying that falling in love is never wrong."

"You're right," she agreed. "I just wish things could have been different."

"We can't change what's happened," I advised her. "All we can do is take what we have and where we are now and make the best of it."

"I feel you," she said. "So, what's up with D and the family? How have things been for you?"

"Okay," I said, hesitantly.

"Just okay?" Tamara pressed. "Come on D, we've known each other for far too long to be giving half-assed answers. What's been up?"

"Nothing, I'm good," I said. Tamara eyed me suspiciously.

"So, I've told you all of my business," she said. "You know how much I spend on booze and drawls, but you want to keep your troubles bottled up? That's not how we gets down. We're better than that."

"You know you're one bottle away from being labeled an alcoholic," I told her.

"Yeah, yeah, yeah and one g-string away from being a

Victoria's Secret model," She said matter of factly. "Don't change the subject. What's up?"

"I'll just say it's days...no weeks, like the ones I've been having lately, that remind me just how much I miss my partner." I said.

"We can't replace him," she said. "If we could, I would have made it happen a long time ago. Even if a chick had to bounce three hundred checks."

"When I find your checkbook, I'm burning it."

"Good luck," she laughed. "But seriously, when you're ready to share with me, I'm willing to listen."

"Thanks Tam," I said appreciatively.

*****

I managed to get somewhat of a grasp on Tamara's spending trends and even got the mess she brought into my office organized and straightened. The good thing about Tamara being slightly clueless about investments and building her stock portfolio was that I could teach her and help her come up with the perfect plan to make her money grow and give her the greatest returns. Although I teased her about her habits every chance I got, the truth was that in my line of work, it's better to start from scratch then to try and correct a mess previously created by a so-call expert.

Tamara hung out in my office for the rest of the day, up until it was time for me to pick up my daughter from daycare. It felt good having a friend around, especially one who reminded me so much of Savoy. Octavia had sent me a text thanking me for the flowers and telling me she would see me when I got home. I was hoping and praying that I would find her and our home in a lot better condition than I had previously. When I entered the kitchen and saw my wife standing over the stove, humming, and cooking, I wanted to fall to my knees and thank the Almighty for answering my prayers!

"Mommy!" Jasmine blurted with excitement.

"Hey baby girl!" Octavia looked refreshed and well rested as she stooped down to eye level with our daughter and gave her a kiss on the cheek. She also looked enticing and sexy in her choice of attire. She wore a short above the knee knit dress that dipped low in the front giving me a peak at her breast. The dress accentuated her hips and highlighted her smooth brown legs. She wore her hair straight and it hung neatly over her shoulders.

"Mommy bought you something," Octavia said to Jasmine.

"Where?" our daughter asked, jumping up and down.

"It's in your room," Octavia answered. "Ask Daddy to take you upstairs to get it."

"Come on," Jasmine said, grabbing my hand.

"I said ask Jazz," Octavia reminded her.

"Please," Jazz looked up at me with her big brown eyes. She knew her please was more than enough. I was a sucker for both of my girls and proud of it.

"Lead the way," I said, patting the top of her head.

"Yayyyy!" Jasmine chanted. I smiled, then looked over at my wife.

"Hurry back," she said sweetly.

Jasmine wasn't the only one who had a surprise waiting for her. The nursery door had been replaced.. I had made arrangements to have someone come out and take care of remodeling, but they weren't coming for another day. It was obvious Octavia had hired someone to beat me to the punch and they had done an excellent job. The walls were now soft blue with eggshell colored trimming. There were new light blue drapes that ran from the top of the window to the floor. As well as a new ceiling fan and even fresh carpet. The crib and other things we purchased in anticipation of our son were gone. I closed the door to the room then waited for Jasmine to accompany me back downstairs. She strolled beside me carrying the purple and pink stringless toy guitar her mother had purchased for her.

"Thank you Mommy," Jasmine said, as the two of us rejoined Octavia in the kitchen.

"You're very welcome," Octavia stated. "Go in the family room until mommy finishes dinner." Jasmine did what she was told. A few seconds later we heard the sounds of what sounded like a cat being skinned alive, but it was actually our daughter making music.

"Are you sure you're ready for that?" I laughed, watching Octavia.

"I got us covered," she said. "We have ear plugs upstairs and when all else fails, we can remove the batteries."

"Sounds good to me," I said. I leaned against the kitchen island watching her maneuver around the stove and the counters. "The room looks nice. I love the color."

"Mama helped pick it out," she said. "After you left this morning, I called her and Daddy and told them what I had planned. They were too happy to help. I really didn't have to do anything but cut the check."

"It still looks nice," I said. "I love it."

"I figure someday the blue will come in handy," she said. She removed the pot she had going on the stove then emptied the contents in the colander she had sitting in the sink.

"What do you mean?"

"We can always try again," she said, softy.

I hadn't even considered the possibility of the two of us someday trying for another child. I guessed there was still a part inside of me that felt guilty over what happened with Josiah. The decision to have another baby was one that took me several months to get Octavia to warm up to. Once she did and the two of us found out she was expecting again she was so happy and anxious. I hated that she got to that point only to have the unthinkable happen.

"Maybe," I said gently. "Someday."

She walked over to me then wrapped her arms around my neck.

"I'm sorry Damon," she said, resting her head on my shoulder. "I was wrong for the way I acted and the things I said." I wrapped my arms around her tightly, holding on and wishing I never had to let her go.

"I'm sorry too," I said. She pulled back then looked

at me.

"Oh, the roses are beautiful," she said. "I put them upstairs in our room. Thank you."

"You're always welcome."

Octavia leaned in and pressed her lips to mine softly. I parted my lips, allowing her tongue to stroke mine. It wasn't until the two of us were mouth to mouth and tongue to tongue that I noticed the faint smell of what I thought to be alcohol on her breath. I decided not to address the subject. Maybe it was mouthwash, I told myself.

Octavia prepared our family a small feast for dinner, consisting of lobster, shrimp, a garden salad, and fresh baked rolls. We prayed together, broke bread together, and then had the pleasure of being serenaded by Jasmine and her new toy. After dinner, Octavia and I gave Jasmine a bath then tucked her in her bed. I ran my hands through Octavia's hair as the two of us lay stretched out across our bed. She lay with her head on my chest and her fingers playing with my close-cut beard.

"How was your day today?" she asked.

"It was good," I said. "Although my evening has been ten times better."

"I'm glad," she said.

"Me too," I said.

"Did you get a chance to talk to Savoy's sister?"

"Yes," I said. I filled her in on my conversations with Tamara and what was currently going on with her and her husband. I also brought her up to speed on my decision to help her get her finances in order.

"She is the poster child for unorganized." I advised her.

"Why? What happened?" Octavia asked. She propped her head up with her arms on my chest.

"Baby, she came to the office with three shoeboxes filled to the brim." I told her. "You should have seen it."

"You know not everyone has our flare for organization."

"I understand that," I said lightly. "But she didn't even have a bank statement."

"Maybe she banks online."

"She couldn't remember the name of her bank," I said seriously.

"How can you not know who has your money?" Octavia frowned.

"That's what I said," I laughed. "She had to pull out her debt card to remember." Octavia laughed.

"Clearly she doesn't have her brother's business sense."

"Not an ounce," I said. "Oh, she mentioned the three of us getting together." I figured since she was the first to bring Tamara up and the conversation was going pleasantly, now was as good of time as ever to hit her with Tamara's request. I'm not a coward, but I'm smart enough to know when and where.

"What about lunch?" she suggested.

I looked down at her blinking my eyes several times. "Really?" I asked surprised.

"Don't look like that," she said. "It's time to put the

bullshit behind us. Savoy and Shontay would want it that way. Besides, maybe we'll discover we have something in common." I continued to stare at her, admiring her beauty while marveling at her wisdom.

"I agree," I said. "And thank you."

"It's true bae," she said. "It's time to repair and heal. Life goes on."

Chapter 13

Octavia

I screwed the top back on the small flask I had
tucked in my purse before I left home. Since I
started taking a shot or two daily, the voices and visions
had stopped plaguing my head. I knew alcohol was
not a permanent solution, and too much consumption
could lead to a shit load of other problems, but I was a
controlled drinker. At least I was since my last drunken
binge. I figured as long as I maintained, I would be fine;
no harm no foul.

I sat in one of the examining rooms of my gynecologist
office, wearing the traditional paper gown, and waiting for
my doctor to come in for my checkup. A minute later,
there was a knock on the exam room door and Doctor
Warren entered carrying a clipboard and folder. Doctor
Warren was an older black man with a receding hair line
and big brown eyes. He had been my OBGYN for several

years and was one of the coolest doctors I had ever met.

"Hey there chicken butt," he smiled, giving me high five.

"Hey doc," I laughed. "How you doing?"

"I'm good," he said, easing down on the rolling stool in the middle of the room. "The question is how are you doing ladybug?"

"I'm doing better," I said. "One day at a time."

"That's the only way we can take it," he said, nodding. "One day at a time." He flipped through several pages on the clipboard, circling different items. "I see you had top notch care when you were in the ER."

"Doctor Aurora?" I asked.

"Yep." He said. "That hubby of yours must have a hook up."

"Why do you say that?" I asked.

"Doctor Mehta Aurora is an excellent physician," Doctor Warren commented, continuing to look at the chart. "He deals mostly with celebrity like clients. Politicians. Reporters. Big names." He looked at me then said, "Not saying that you and Damon don't fit the mold—"

"I know what you're saying," I said. I wanted him to know there was no need to explain and that I was in no way offended. "I thought he just worked at the hospital."

"No," he said. "Huntsville Hospital is a public hospital and if Aurora is at a public hospital, it's because he's been requested."

I thought about Doctor Warren's words briefly, then dismissed them without a second thought. The rest of my visit went well and I was given the go ahead to resume my normal sexual activity. I was happy to hear this, but I knew Damon was going to be ecstatic. The two of us agreed to meet for lunch at the Ambiance where Tamara would also be joining us. I meant what I told Damon about it being time to repair and heal, and I was ready for all of us to move on.

I still had a little more than an hour until we were scheduled for our lunch date, but I arrived early for an interview Marilyn had scheduled for me. I had been keeping up with the functions and the daily operations from my home office and both Tabitha and Marilyn were doing an excellent job, but it was time for me to solidify a replacement for Amel and get Tabitha back on a regular eight-hour schedule. As usual, my employees were happy to see me and appeared to be getting along. I made my rounds through the dining room, the lounge, and the kitchen before slipping into my office. As soon as my butt hit my chair, Tabitha knocked on the door.

"Hey now," she said entering the room. "How are you feeling?"

"Hey Tab, I'm good." I said. "How are you?"

"Busy and loving it," she said cheerfully.

"I'm happy to hear that," I said.

"Are you expecting a visitor?" she asked. "There's a gentleman waiting for you in the dining room." The applicant Marilyn selected for me was a man name Joe Santo. Joe and Marilyn had worked together at her previous place of employment.

"I'm actually expecting three today," I advised her. "Joe Santo is my first, then I have a lunch date with my hubby and a friend."

"Well, Mr. Santo is already here," Tabitha told me. "Would you like me to send him in?"

My interview with Joe wasn't for another forty minutes. I had already been wowed by his resume and his reference from Marilyn. He was now batting a thousand with his punctuality.

"Yes, please do," I said. I reached down in my bag and pulled out my leather binder that contained the resume Marilyn had faxed me at home. Joe was a tall, nicely built, olive-skinned man with light green eyes and dark silky hair. He wore a nice business suit and an emerald green tie. After speaking with him about his ten years of experience in restaurant management, I was not only impressed, but convinced he was the right man for the job. I held my breath when I told him about the criminal background check and drug test. I'd had my share of applicants who cringed at the mere mention of both, but Joe didn't blink twice. After giving him the drug testing form, I shook his hand and advised him I would be in touch. If everything came back clear with Joe, I planned to offer him a position and get him started within the next seven days. I decided that giving Tabitha a raise was also necessary and well deserved. I called her into my office to commend her on a job well done and to let her know that she would see the increase on her upcoming check.

"I can't thank you enough for your dedication and your loyalty," I said. "You and the rest of the team have been exceptional."

"It's our job," she said. "We're happy to do it."

"Well, I wanted to let you know again none of it has gone unnoticed and I'm giving you a raise," I said smiling. Tabitha's eyes lit up while she looked at me.

"Are you serious?" She asked.

"Very," I said. "You can expect to see it on your next check. I thought an additional two dollars an hour would be a good start."

"An hour?" she repeated. Tabitha looked completely stumped from the news.

"Yes, an hour," I said.

"Oh," she said frowning. "I thought General Managers were salaried."

"General Managers are salaried," I said. "My Lead Hostess all get paid by the hour."

"Wow," she said, "I assumed with the performance I've been giving these last few weeks that the position was now mine."

"Tab, I'm sorry, but my criteria for the position hasn't changed," I said. "I think—"

"I've been doing the same job that Amel did," she stated. "And I'm doing the same job Marilyn's doing," she said, cutting me off. "What other criteria is necessary?"

"I agree you have been doing much of the same task but—"

"But what?" she questioned, cutting me off again. "I

do the orders, I work the floor. I keep the traffic coming. I do that!"

"Tabitha, who does the payroll?" I questioned. "The schedule? Prepares the menus? Handles marketing and promotions?" I was by no means trying to downplay what Tabitha was doing, I was only trying to differentiate between her tasks and everything that went into keeping us in business.

"So let me try!" she snapped. "I can handle it Octavia, and right now we both know you ca—"

The look I was giving her must have been the red flag she needed to halt the insult I felt was coming. I folded my hands in front of me on the desk while gathering my words. *"Bitch, don't overplay your stroke"* was clearly the wrong choice of words, but they were the only ones I was thinking at that moment!

"I thank you for being discreet about my breakdown that day in the parking lot," I said firmly. "I thank you for going the extra mile out of the way for these last few weeks, but please don't forget that it's my name on your check, and long before *my* customers or *my* staff even knew you existed, *I* was turning a profit and bringing in traffic."

"You have passed me over for this position twice," she said, holding up two fingers. "When Amel was strung out and treating her veins, you hired me and I bust my ass to prove myself, but yet you let her come back and then promoted her!"

"Leave Amel out of this," I said through clenched

teeth. "And if I remember correctly when I hired you back then this was the first job you had in years. You couldn't handle the demands that came along with the job."

"So why did you hire Marilyn?" she demanded.

It was my right not to justify any of my business decisions to anyone but God, but I chose to answer the questions Tabitha was dropping before me.

"Because she was qualified," I said frankly. "Ambiance 2 does almost three times what we do here. I wanted someone with previous management experience who could handle the crowd and the rush."

"Is it because she was qualified or because she's black?"

No, the hell she didn't! I thought.

"It's because her resume was worthy," I said offended. "Nothing more or less. I understand you feel that you should have been offered the position, but after this conversation it's clear I made the right choice then and that I'm making the right choice once again. Now, if you don't understand that or you feel that you deserve something other than what I've presented here, feel free to clock out and go home."

She stood looking at me with low, dark eyes. I stood waiting for her to say whatever it was she was feeling or if she was feeling lucky—to make the wrong move; either way the ball was in her court and I was down for whatever.

"I think I'll return to my post now," she said. "Thank

you for the raise and for the talk." She turned on her heels then walked out the room leaving the door open behind her. I picked up the phone and called Ambiance 2 to ask Marilyn if she knew of one more potential applicant for a hostess position. After the conversation I had with Tabitha, I had a nudging feeling that soon I would be replacing another employee.

*****

"Octavia, I'm glad we could get together," Tamara said, looking at me from across the table. The two of us, along with Damon sat in one of the leather booths close to my office. Although Tabitha's attitude had improved tremendously since our discussion, I wanted to stay close to the office so I could watch her every move. I didn't think she was stupid enough to try something crazy, but at the same time I never thought she would throw the race card at me either.

I watched Tamara while thinking to myself that the way she favored Savoy was almost uncanny. They had the same pecan-colored skin and bright smile.

"I am too," I said truthfully.

"I'm sorry for how me and my sisters and mother reacted towards Shontay," she said. "We were overprotective and stupid."

I agree, I thought to myself. "No worries," I said. "It's a new day."

Tamara smiled, while Damon squeeze my knee under the table. I listened to the two of them talk about the misadventures of Damon and Savoy while we waited on our food. When Tabitha brought our order, all conversation ceased within an instant and we all dug in.

"Girl, this is good," Tamara commented. She order the chicken penne pasta while Damon and I had the honey-glazed blackened chicken with mixed vegetables.

"Thank you," I said appreciatively.

"You are very welcome," Tamara said. "Says me and my stomach." She laughed then continued to eat.

I sipped on my lemon water while she and Damon talked about the rest of her family. As our meal progressed I started to feel somewhat like a window shopper peeking into their conversation. When Kaitlyn came by to refresh our beverages, I asked her to bring me a sweet tea. If I could have gotten away with something stronger I would have, but tea would have to do it for the moment.

I looked from Tamara to Damon watching how her eyes lit up with every word he said, how she laughed at all of his jokes, and appeared to hang on his every word. I sipped my drink slowly while wondering if there was more that she wanted then just to have a friendship with Damon and me. *You can't trust theses bitches,* a voice in my head said. The more Tamara spoke, the more her voice began to irritate me. It was like someone was dragging their nails across a chalk board; flesh-crawling and annoying.

"Damon…" she whined. "D," she purred. *"Why does she keep calling his name?"* the voice asked. *"She reminds me of Lena."* I could feel my nerves shriveling to the point of collapsing, I decided to excuse myself from the table. "I'll be right back," I said quickly.

"Okay babe," Damon replied. I slid out the booth and walked quickly to my office. Inside the office I shut the door then grabbed my purse.

"You know she wants your man," the voice said. *"Everybody wants Damon…you better go handle that bitch!"*

"Shut up!" I demanded. "Shut up now!"

I pulled out the flask I had in my bag, unscrewed the top, then took a long sip until the flask was empty. I screwed the top back on then dropped the flask back in my purse.

"Remember Nadia?" the voice continued. *"She wanted to be Damon's friend too."*

The voice continued to speak to me, reminding me of the women who had desperately tried to ruin my marriage. *"I bet that's why she never liked Shontay,"* it said. *"Shontay knew she wanted your man."*

I stood with my back facing the door and my hands grabbing the edge of my desk. I could hear myself breathing heavily but there was no way to stop it. The voice kept speaking to me and with her every word my anger began to boil. There was a light tap on my office door.

"Who is it?" I asked through clenched teeth.

"It's me Tamara," Tamara said from the other side of the door.

"Damon's not enough Octavia," the voice chanted. *"I bet she wants your daughter too. I bet she wants your daughter too."*

I looked down watching as the perspiration that dripped from my face fell onto the back of my hands.

"Come in," I said, taking a deep breath.

"Girl, I have got to go but I want to thank you for lunch," she said, "It was the bomb!"

"It was my pleasure," I said, almost breathless.

"You okay?" she asked. I could feel her moving closer.

"Let her know Octavia, after all she did ask!"

"No," I said, standing up straight. I tugged on the hem of my suit jacket then turned on my heels to face Tamara only to find Lena staring back at me. She stood in the middle of my office floor with her lips puckered and a look of satisfaction on her face. "You mutherfucking bitch! " I yelled, charging towards her.

Chapter 14

Damon

I slid out the booth quickly when I heard Octavia's voice. I, along with several of Octavia's employees, ran straight for the office. I was in disbelief when I found Octavia and Tamara on the office floor engaged in a brawl. I'm talking hair pulling, shirts ripped, and fist swinging. Although Tamara was the bigger of the two of them it was obvious that my wife was dominating the fight. She sat on her ass pulling Tamara's hair with one hand and hitting her in the face with the other.

"Stop it!" I yelled, moving in closer. I grabbed Octavia from behind wrapping my arms around her waist pulling her up to her feet. "Let her go! Now!"

"Stay away from my husband you dirty ass hoe!" Octavia screamed, kicking Tamara wherever she could land her heels.

"Get off me you crazy bitch!" Tamara yelled, swinging

back. She was practically crawling on her knees due to Octavia still having a grip on the woman's hair. Octavia held on with her right hand, while continuing to swing and with her left. The more I tried to pull her away, the tighter her grip became. One of the bus boys pushed through the crowd of spectators now standing at the door and managed to pry Octavia's fingers open to free Tamara. Once he did, I grabbed both her arms restraining her. Tamara pulled herself up to her feet with her fist balled. I stepped in front of my wife, facing her.

"I said stop it now!" I ordered. Tamara's chest rose and fell quickly as she looked at me. Her hair stood up on one side and there was a large welt underneath her left eye. The silk shirt she wore was ripped across the sleeve. She looked at me again then turned on her heels marching through the crowd.

"You heard him hoe," Octavia babbled from behind me. "Fallback before I beat that ass again!"

I spun around looking at her. "Do I need to remind you where we are?" I asked, staring at her.

"No, but you need to remind her!" Octavia snapped.

I could smell the liquor on her breath. This time there was no denying it. I adjusted the jacket of my suit then looked at the employees and customers who were watching us.

"Please return to what you were doing," I said, as professionally as possible. "Immediately."

"Let's go," Tabitha ordered, motioning to the crowd. "Show's over." She looked at Octavia, shook her head then shut the office door.

"Where is it?" I asked, walking around to the desk.

"Where's...where's what?" she asked. It was like she had done a complete 360.

"You're drunk," I said angrily. I pulled out every drawer that was unlocked looking for the evidence. I knew the only way my wife could be tipsy was because she had something hidden.

"I'm not drunk!" she snapped, watching me.

I ignored the lie I knew she was telling and continued my search. When I came up empty handed I grabbed her handbag. I dumped out all the contents on the desk, watching as the silver plated flask landed among Octavia's possessions. I picked up the empty container then held it in front of her face.

"What in the hell are you thinking!" I demanded. "What is wrong with you?" She stared at me with a glazed and confused look on her face.

"Deny it now!" I barked. "Go ahead Octavia. Deny it!"

"I don't know what happened," she stuttered. "I kept hearing this voice and I saw...I saw—"

"Save it!" I said disgusted. "How many days?"

"How many days what?"

"How many days have you been getting drunk?"

"I'm not drunk!" she argued. "I drink so they'll stop..."
I wondered if she could hear herself. If she believed the things that she was saying. I wondered who the woman standing in front of me was and what she had done with

the woman I loved.

"Get your things," I said, tired of her excuses. "Let's go!"

*****

I pulled around to the back of my home then shoved the gearshift in to park. I killed the engine then got out slamming the door behind me. I didn't bother opening the door for Octavia, I was on a mission. I opened the door to our home leaving it open behind me. I disarmed the alarm then stumped over to the kitchen cabinet and swung the door open.

"Damon," Octavia called my name.

I ignored her then continued with my assignment. I pulled every bottle of wine and liquor from the cabinet and sat them on the counter.

"What are you doing?" Octavia asked.

"Something I should have done a long time ago," I said. I opened and popped the corks on every single bottle then poured the contents down the drain two bottles at a time.

"Damon," she said, walking up to me. "Why are you doing this? The drinking isn't the problem. I told you...I told you what was happening..."

"What Octavia?" I asked, slamming down two bottles then picking up another two. "That the voices are making you do it? That they make you drink?"

"Yes," she said. "Yes."

"Bull shit," I said, turning to face her. "You drink

because you want to. You drink because rather than facing the fact that our son is dead, you would rather wallow in self-pity and bring down every one around you!"

"I don't need a reminder of what happened to my son," she snapped back. "I carried him and I almost died getting him here."

I ignored her remarks while emptying out the last two bottles.

"Where were you Damon?" she screamed, pushing me. "You want to save me now! Where were you when I needed you then?"

I stopped what I was doing by throwing the bottles in the steel sink. The force of the impact caused the last two bottles to bust.

"I came as soon as I could," I said, with my back to her. "As soon as I knew. I can't change that."

I was hurt by her words. What Octavia didn't know was that I had been blaming myself ever since that day and silently telling myself that I could have prevented everything that happened. I had been reminding myself that if I hadn't been so obsessed with love for her, half of the bad shit that happened to her would have never taken place; including the loss of Savoy and Shontay.

"You should have moved faster," she taunted.

I clinched my fist, feeling the burning sensation of rage as it flowed through my body. I inhaled through my nose then slowly exhaled through my lips attempting to manage my anger. I failed.

"I'll tell you where I wasn't," I said, spinning around

and looking at her. "I wasn't laying on my ass sloppy drunk, playing make believe, like you were when you should have been taking care of our daughter." I paused staring at her. "But then I really shouldn't be that surprised with your behavior, we both know whenever there is something too heavy for you to deal with, your first stop is by a bottle. At least this time you didn't take that bottle and run to another man."

My mentioning the day Octavia had a breakdown when she discovered her mother had cancer was a low and childish blow, but at that second I didn't give a damn. She looked at me with her eyes wide and her lips slightly open then pulled back her hand and slapped me hard in the face.

"You go to hell," she said, shaking while she backed away from me.

"What do you think you've been putting me through?" I asked. I walked off then out the door.

I sat behind the wheel of my car, driving in the direction of my office, while attempting to process the things that had taken place throughout the day between me and my wife. I felt defeated and lost without a clue of how I was going to get the two of us back to the place where we belonged. I was willing to fight against any and every principality Octavia and I faced, but I couldn't and would no longer attempt to fight alone. I picked up my cell phone and dialed Tamara's number.

"Hello," she answered with attitude.

"Can we talk?" I asked, ignoring the anger in her

voice.

"I don't have time for other people's drama," she ranted. "Trust me, if I wanted that I got plenty of that back in Atlanta. For real."

"I'm not trying to pull you into any," I said. "I would never do that, but I would like to talk." *Silence.*

"Please Tam," I said. "Right now you're the closest thing I have to a friend."

"Where you at?" she asked.

"On my way back to the office," I said.

"Nope," she said quickly. "Not there. That could be a setup."

"Where?"

"Highland Pointe," she said. "196 Jeff..."

*****

Tamara opened the door to her apartment wearing grey shorts and a grey *Crimson Tide* t-shirt. The welt underneath her eye had gone down revealing the scratch Octavia had put there. She stepped back from the door allowing me to step inside. I glanced around the living room admiring the retro style furniture and décor before sitting on the bright red sofa against the living room wall. Tamara sat down on the sofa next to me then turned facing me. I had it made up in my mind that I would open up and tell my friend about my thoughts, feelings, and even the death of my son, but when I opened my mouth to begin no words came, instead the only thing I shared was my misery and regret in the form of tears.

"Damon," Tamara said moving in closer to me. I dropped my face in my hands to cover my vulnerability, but everything I had pushed back, every fear and every strand of guilt pushed through leaving me open. Tamara put her arms around me allowing me to rest my head against her breast.

"Shh..." she said, stroking my hair. "It's okay...it's okay."

I cried like a child with no pride; like a man with no shame. "I'm sorry," I said through my tears. "I'm sorry..." I sat up then wiped the tears from my eyes with the back of my hands. Once I felt like I could speak without breaking down, I shared with her the details of what Octavia and I had been going through. I didn't stop there. I told her about the pain I felt when Savoy was murdered and how hard it was for me to deal with it. I opened up and poured out my heart and Tamara listened without interruption. When my confession was complete, I exhaled, feeling like the weight of a three-story building had been lifted off my shoulders. I sat on the edge of the sofa staring down at my hands.

"I'm sorry for this," I said, referring to my emotional outburst.

"Look at me Damon," she said. She stroked my cheek with her fingertips. "Look at me." I slowly raised my head doing as she requested. She looked at me with compassion and understanding. "It's okay," she said. "Baby you have nothing to be sorry about. The best men cry and feel pain. It's okay."

She brushed her index finger over my cheek again. There was a foreign tension in the air around us, one that I never anticipated would ever develop between me and the woman I knew as my friend. The silky feel of her fingertips stroking my face over and over again turned from soothing to sensual as she leaned in allowing our lips to meet. She pulled away looking at me with eyes that looked as if they were asking me for permission. When I didn't protest, she pressed her lips to mine again. I reciprocated allowing my tongue to dominate hers while my hand slipped in between her legs. I pulled myself up using the weight of my body to push her back against the arm of the couch. She spread her legs allowing me to assume position in between them. Our tongues played intimately while my hands caressed and massaged her breast. I felt my nature rising with every kiss and every stroke of her warm wet tongue. As the two of us continued to engage our lips, I allowed the yearning pushing against the inside of my crotch to overshadow the reasoning inside my mind.

G STREET CHRONICLES
A NEW URBAN DYNASTY

WWW.GSTREETCHRONICLES.COM

Chapter 15

Octavia

I was embarrassed and humiliated by the events that had taken place in front of my customers and staff, but what hurt me more so was that even after I told Damon the truth about what had been going on with me, he didn't believe me. I could handle his anger. I could even handle his disappointment, but I couldn't handle the thought of him no longer believing in me.

I sat behind the wheel of Damon's Land Rover, outside of the ABC store. Damon had poured out everything we kept in our home, but he couldn't stop me from using my money. I grabbed my bag and phone and climbed out my car walking towards the store. I was halfway inside the store when my phone began to ring. I pressed the end call button assuming it was Damon, sending the call to voicemail. A second later my phone rang again. I rushed through the glass doors of the store while glancing at my caller ID, the name Stanley Security appeared on my display.

"Hello," I answered.

"This is Jonah from Stanley Security I'm looking for Mrs. Whitmore."

"This is Octavia," I replied.

"Mrs. Whitmore can you please verify your billing address?"

"For my home or office?" I asked annoyed. "You monitor both."

"For the Ambiance," the young man said.

"Yes, it's 2099 Main Street."

"Thank you for verifying and if you don't mind can you verify your pin?"

"You called me," I said loudly. "Why do you need me to verify? You should have my information there!" The cashiers behind the registers inside the store looked at me. I wanted to tell them to mind their business but decided against it.

"Mrs. Whitmore verification is for your protection," Jonah said calmly.

"It's 9869," I said, reminding myself that he was right.

"Thank you for verifying," he said. "Mrs. Whitmore I'm calling to notify you that the monitors in Zone 4 is still offline." The area of the Ambiance referred to as Zone 4 was my office. I originally only had my offices wired with cameras, but after my kidnapping Damon and I agreed it would be good to include cameras that viewed each of the exits as well.

"What do you mean by still?" I asked.

"It's been offline now for over a month."

"A month? Are you serious? Why didn't I get a call when it first when offline?" I questioned.

"Actually, ma'am, you did."

"Actually, no I didn't," I said sarcastically. I scanned the stocked shelves with my eyes while attempting to decide on my poison for the day. I finally decided to go with my old faithful, better known as *Ciroc*. I grabbed the first flavor I saw then strolled to the counter.

"Mrs. Whitmore we called the Ambiance and spoke with the manager on the first, and the fifteenth of this month, as well as the first day we noticed a problem. We were advised that you were working on getting some of your wiring replaced. We also sent you a courtesy email."

Tabitha, I thought. She had been such a smartass earlier telling me all the shit she was handling but it was obvious she was coming up short on what was important.

"We offered to send a technician out, but the offer was declined," he informed me.

"Why are you just calling me?" I asked.

"We were advised you were in the hospital." he said. "I called today and spoke with someone by the name of Heather who advised me she was unaware of a problem and suggested I call your emergency contact number we have on file." I paused thinking about what Jonah was stating. Why hadn't Tabitha alerted me of a problem? Why hadn't she allowed Stanley to send out a tech?

"Jonah what day did you say the monitor first went

offline?" I asked.

"$32.98," the heavy set, redhead whispered to me. I held up my finger indicating I wanted her to wait. She rolled her eyes impatiently then folded her arms across her sagging breast.

"On July tenth," Jonah stated. July the tenth was a day I could never forget even if I wanted. It was the day I went into labor and the same day Amel passed.

"Jonah can you tell me who your rep spoke with that morning?"

"One moment...Yes ma'am, that morning we also spoke with the manager, Tabitha Bachman."

"$32.98" the cashier repeated again. I dug in my purse, removed two crisp twenty dollar bills and dropped them on the counter before grabbing my bag and walking out the door.

"Jonah can you get a tech out to my restaurant today?" I asked, getting back into my car.

"Let me check," he said. I heard him tapping on keys the sound of a mouse clicking. "I can't, but I can get someone out between one and five tomorrow."

"That will be fine," I said. I was pissed that Tabitha hadn't notified me of a problem with the camera, but now I had additional backing if she tried to hit me with some more of her, "is it because I'm not black" nonsense.

I pulled out of the parking lot headed for my home when my phone chirped, advising me that I had missed voicemails. I pressed *86 on my phone, then replayed the messages. No matter how hurt or angry I was with my husband, I was hoping that one of my messages was from him; they weren't. The most recent one was Kaitlyn advising me that Stanley Security had been trying to reach me. I scanned through listening until I came across a message from Betty Fletcher.

"Thank you so much for the check," she said. "Again I appreciate it." I felt a wave of guilt for the way I had inadvertently been brushing Amel's mother off. The woman had lost her daughter; her only child. Her pain had to be astronomical. I rode down the interstate thinking about Amel and all the laughs the two of us shared, from the time we spent together while planning her nuptials with Tarik, to the days we worked side by side in the restaurant, busting our tails. The two of us had been through our ups and our downs, but she always came through when I needed her, in fact she was the one who told Damon that she saw Gator in the restaurant the day he had me kidnapped. She had given Damon and my father the lead they needed to track me down. I hit the dial pad on my phone then called Amel's mother.

"Hello."

"Hi Ms. Fletcher, it's Octavia Whitmore."

"Hey Ms. Octavia," she said. "I've been thinking about you."

"I'm sorry," I said. "I've been a little out the loop." I said ashamed.

"It's okay sweetie," she said. "How have you been feeling?"

"I'm okay Ms. Fletcher, "I lied.

"Just okay?" she asked. There was a certain something in her voice, telling me she was reading through what I said and what I had not.

"Yes ma'am," I said lowly. "Just feeling bad that I haven't reached out to you personally."

"Don't feel bad suga. You know I know all about losing your child," she said gently. "Especially unexpectedly. I think it's one thing when you know their sick and God's been preparing you for what's to come and it's another when it happens overnight."

"I agree, but I think our cases are a little different," I said. "You had a lot more time invested. I imagine what you're dealing with his a lot harder."

"Loss is loss," she said. "Your child is your child. It doesn't matter if it's for twenty-nine years or only for a day."

"Thank you," I said sighing. "But I didn't call to worry you with my problems. I called to talk about you."

"You're not worrying me," she said. "I love to talk and talking is good. So, is listening because when you listen it reminds you that you're not alone." I felt a small lump sitting in the middle of my throat as tears began to form in my eyes.

"I've been feeling like that lately," I admitted. "Alone and like I was losing my mind. I don't know what's wrong with me."

"Grief can do that," she said. "It's just like hate Octavia…it'll consume you if you let it. That's why we have to let things out. When I found out my baby was dead, I cried so hard you could have sworn the roof was shaking. I cried every day until we buried her and then when we did, I cried some more…but then I decided I was going to talk about it. So, I found me one person who would listen and I started to feel better. Don't get me wrong, I still cry. Sweetie, I cried yesterday. I even cried today and I'll probably cry tomorrow, but at least I'm letting it out."

I started to feel pressure building inside of me as I continued to focus on the road in front of me. "I think one of the hardest things for me is that when I saw him, it was like I was looking at a stranger," I cried opening up. "What kind of mother feels that way? I carried him for eight months and I know I loved him, but when I saw him…I was numb, but ever since I've been feeling like something wasn't right and in my head things have been completely wrong. I can't even remember it all…"

"Octavia, there's nothing wrong with you," she said. "Maybe you're just depressed…it happens all the time, it's just a lot of our folk don't like to talk about it until it's too late. I'm convinced that's what happened to Amel. She probably was still upset about her break up with Tarik. I imagine she got to thinking and hearing her own voices and then she made a real bad decision…and once again got caught up with the wrong crowd."

"The wrong crowd?" I asked, curious. "What do you mean?"

"Those people like that boy Beau she use to date," she said with distaste. I was always afraid that Amel would fall back to her old habits, but I really never had any evidence or anything to validate my feelings. I didn't know all of Amel's friends and associates, but the one's that did come around were far from the kind of person Beau was; or at least that's what I thought.

"Ms. Fletcher how do you know?"

"The night before her accident, one of them came down here," she said. "He told me he was a friend of Amel's and that he was just checking on me to make sure I was all right. I opened the door because he looked like a nice man. He was tall and well dressed in a suit and those expensive shoes. He said his name was Diago or Deshon or something like that. I thought maybe Amel had gotten herself a new boyfriend. Well, then he called Amel on the phone and told her I wanted to speak to her, so I said hi, but then before she could respond he snatched the phone back and left. I called Amel after that and something didn't sound right about her. She said she was okay, but I knew better and now she's dead."

"Ms. Fletcher, I don't think Amel was back on drugs," I said. "I think she may have slipped off the curb." I knew what I saw that day, Amel had intentionally walked in front of the car, but I was trying, in a way, to give the woman comfort and solace even if it was coming from a lie. There was a long gap of silence on the other end of the phone. "Ms. Fletcher?"

"I wish that was true Octavia," she said. "But that's not what the autopsy report says. They found traces of LSD in her blood. Octavia, she was high."

*****

After my conversation with Ms. Fletcher I was curious and concerned. She mentioned that the man who came to see her was well dressed and wore expensive shoes; the first person that came to mind was Gator. I knew it was physically impossible considering he was in prison, but the man had connections all over the state and probably the country. I thought back, remembering the dream I had of him the morning that my life took such a dramatic change. Maybe it was a warning, but what did it all mean? I sat in my home office staring at the flat screen monitor, Goggling the drug LSD. The results it brought up advised me the drug was a hallucinogen. The vivid image of Amel standing on the sidewalk staring at the building replayed in my head. I remembered how strange her behavior had been. Amel wasn't trying to kill herself; she was on a bad trip that sadly she didn't make it back from. I had temporarily forgotten the issues with the security system at my restaurant. I closed the internet browser then grabbed the cordless phone I had sitting on my desk; calling the Ambiance.

"Kaitlyn," I said, cutting her off before she could finish her greeting. "Is Tabitha around?"

"No ma'am, she went on a bank run."

"Okay, do me a favor…" I gave Kaitlyn instructions on how to check the camera in my office, then waited on hold for her while she did so. Several minutes later she returned.

"Sorry it took me so long," she said winded. "All the

wires looked fine to me."

"Thank you Kaitlyn."

"No problem."

"Um, one more thing," I said quickly. "Do you remember anything out of the ordinary about Amel the day she died? Was she acting strange or different?"

"Not really," she said. "We were super busy so I really didn't get to talk to her, but she looked okay. I mean she came in then she went straight to the office with Tabitha and your friend."

"What friend?"

"I don't know her name, but you know her, I've see you talking to her too…she's short and a little on the heavy side." I thought for a moment.

"Shayla?" I asked confused.

"I guess," she said. "I saw her in the booth with you. That was the day you left early because you were sick." I knew Kaitlyn was referring to the day I had my panic attack.

"Are you sure she went straight to my office?"

"I'm positive," she said confidently.

"Thanks Kaitlyn," I said.

"Octavia," she said.

"Yes?"

"I'm sorry about what happened to you," she said solemnly. "I've wanted to tell you that—"

"Thank you Kaitlyn," I said.

"Are you okay?" she asked nervously.

"I'm getting there," I said.

"Good. By the way, I saw what happened today."
I cringed from the thought of having to explain my behavior earlier to her and the rest of my staff, but part of being a true leader is owning up and admitting your mistakes.

"I'm sorry that you had to see me like that Kaitlyn. I was wrong for my behavior and you have my word it will ever happen again."

"It's okay," she said, loudly. "I respect a woman having to put a b…I mean, another woman in check."

I reminded myself that Kaitlyn was one of my younger employees I had on staff and probably thought that I was justified for snapping. The tone of her voice told me that she probably would have jumped in.

"Thank you," I said, suppressing my urge to laugh. "But there is a way to do everything and clearly I chose the wrong path."

"Well, we still love you," she said.

"And I love all of you." I said before hanging up.

My first thought was to call Tabitha and question her on what Kaitlyn had advised me, but I decided to hold off until I spoke to Shayla. I knew the connection with the two of them could possibly be nothing more than a coincidence and Kaitlyn could have mistaken the two women bumping into each other for friendship, but I needed to be a hundred percent sure. I decided I would give Shayla a call tomorrow to find out for myself. In the meantime, I needed to try and smooth out the problems with my husband.

Chapter 16

Damon

Octavia sent me a text stating that she had already picked Jasmine up from daycare and that she was going to visit with her parents. I replied with a short and simple, "Ok." At that moment I didn't know what else to say, I was standing in Tamara's living room putting my clothes back on and trying hard not to think about what she and I had just done.

"So what happens now?" Tamara asked, as the two of us stood by her front door. I didn't want to have that conversation with her, but I knew I couldn't run out with any discussion at all. The two of us had crossed a line that we couldn't come back from and I allowed it. Now I had to deal with the questions and consequences like a man.

"I'm going home," I said gently. "To my daughter and my wife."

"There wasn't a doubt in my mind that you were doing that," she said giving me a small smirk.

I could see it in her eyes that she was open to the possibility of something more. I wasn't. I had allowed my dick to do the thinking for me, and now I was standing in front of a woman whom I'd known for years trying to find a polite way to let her know that what the two of us just did was nothing more than a one-night stand.

"Tamara I didn't mean to take advantage of you," I said, "I just got caught up."

She looked at me and frowned. "Don't do that," she said.

"Do what?"

"Apologize," she said. "When a man apologizes to a woman after they have sex and says he took advantage of her even though the act was consensual between two grown ass people...it's just another way of saying that woman was a pity fuck."

"Tam, that's not what this was," I said honestly. "I think we were both in need of something."

"To get laid," she said bluntly.

"No, "I said. "There's an emotional connection between the two of us and somewhere in the process those emotions turned physical...we gave in."

"D, you don't have to take the long road to a pit stop," she said. "Let's call it for what it is or what it was. You have regrets and it'll never happen again."

I paused then nodded my head agreeing with her.

"So again I ask," she said. "Where do we go from

here?"

"Back to friends," I said.

"I'll take that," she said casually.

I was slightly grateful that I beat Octavia home. I needed to shower and I wanted some time to myself before I had to deal with her attitude. I stood in the shower allowing the hot, pulsating water to beat across my skin while thinking about the day's events. I had made the ultimate mistake, and now not only had I possibly ruined a friendship, but I had yet another thing to feel guilty about. In my own temporary moment of insanity, the thought came to me to just come clean with Octavia. However, as soon as I turned off the faucet that thought went down the drain with the soap suds. There was no way in hell I was going to tread those waters. It was a guarantee I would drown. I know my conscious wouldn't be clear, but I'd rather ride with a dirty conscious with my wife beside me, than to have a clean one and ride alone.

I grabbed a thick towel off the shelf and dried my body off before finally securing the towel around my waist. When I opened the bathroom door, I was surprised to see Octavia sitting on the edge of the bed wearing a red fitted tank dress and sandals. Her hair was secured on top of her head with several curls surrounding her face.

"Hi," she said, watching me.

"Hey," I replied. I walked over to the armoire then pulled out the drawer, removing a pair of shorts and a t-shirt. I kept my back to her as I slipped each of them on.

"You know one of the things I commend my Dad for is that when he was an alcoholic he had the courage to walk away from me and Mama," she sighed. "It takes a very courageous person to walk away from everything you know and the ones you love so that you don't subject others to your bullshit."

I turned around then looked at her. I was confused on where she was going with our conversation. "I always said that someday I would be that kind of person. That I would leave you and Jazz before I took you through hell."

"Octavia—"

"Let me finish," she said. "I know what I did today and the day I forgot to pick up Jazz was bad. I know my emotions have been up and down and up again. I know that you have been keeping your feelings and thoughts to yourself for fear that I couldn't handle it and because you were too busy worrying about me. I know I've been screwed up since Josiah..."

It was the first time I heard her call him by his name.

"...died," she continued. "And I know right now what I should do is pack my bags and have the courage to walk away, but the truth is at times, I'm a little selfish and to be real...I'm not that brave." She stood and walked up to me. "So no matter how crazy I may be right now or how hard this is, we are stuck with each other Damon and there isn't a damn thing either of us can do about that. Baby, I'm so sorry for the things I said and I know you would do anything you could to protect and save me. I know that and I thank you for that." She stared at me through her beautiful brown eyes as tears slowly rolled down her cheeks. "I love you Damon and no matter what we go through or how we go through it…that love will always remain the same, but I need you to believe in me." She shook as her tears poured rapidly. "I need you to believe in me because if you don't…if you don't then…"

I reached out and grabbed her, pulling her against my chest. "I do believe in you." I whispered, kissing the top of her head. "I believed in you the first moment I saw you and I knew I loved you even then. I am so sorry baby for everything I said and all that I've done." I was not only talking about the mistakes she was aware of but my recent infidelity. "You make me better," I continued. "You make me good and you truly are the best thing that has ever happened to me. I love you and I would lay down my life for you and Jazz. No questions asked."

Octavia raised her head looking at me like she was staring through to my soul. I saw a longing and a craving in her corneas that had been gone for far too long.

"I need you," she said, cupping my face in her hands.

"I'm right here," I whispered. She kissed my lips with force and passion. I could feel the adrenaline rushing through my veins as my heart beat increased with every growing inch of my dick. I grabbed the back of her head, allowing my fingers to get tangled in the soft strands of hair, while backing her up against the bed. Octavia's hand grabbed, then squeeze the soldier standing in between my legs, as I pulled my hands from her hair, down her back until I was cupping the cheeks of her ass.

She pushed gently on my chest, causing me to take a step back, and then dropped to her knees. In less than two seconds my shorts were around my ankles and her lips were covering my shaft. My knees buckled as Octavia bobbed up and down, sucking me like I was made of edible chocolate. She pulled back then stood and kissed me again. I grabbed the hem of her dress, pulling it up and over her head before tossing the material to the floor. I marveled at every inch of her skin, I longed for every ounce of her curves as she climbed onto the bed then motioned for me. I removed the rest of my clothing as I climbed on to the bed, ready to return to the home that I knew was mine and mine only. I suppressed my urge to dive in and instead pushed each of her legs back with my hands. I rotated my tongue against the hood of her clit, inhaling her natural aroma, then sucked on her pleasure knob. I slid my tongue in and out then up and down her warm, wet opening before sliding my index finger in.

Octavia moaned passionately as I massaged her clit in between my lips. "Damon..." she groaned, grabbing my head. I dipped my finger in and out while licking then sucking then licking on Octavia's engorged clit until her legs shook uncontrollably and her wetness overflowed. I assumed the position in between her legs, slowly easing my way into her hot tight hole. The walls of her pussy hugged my dick as Octavia rotated her hips, throwing it back at me. She wrapped her legs around my waist, holding me tight. I pushed further going deeper inside her pussy, feeding her all of my dick until I felt the joy in the pit of my stomach and every muscle in my body became stiff. I came strong and hard; filling Octavia's inner kingdom and letting the walls to her lower city know that Daddy was home.

Chapter 17

Octavia

I saw my husband off for work then showered, dressed, and prepared to take care of some business of my own. The first thing on my agenda was reaching out to Shayla. I retrieved the business card she had given me the last time the two of us saw each other, then tried the number from my cellphone. I was surprised when I was greeted by an automated message informing me that the number I had dialed was no longer in service. I checked the number, as the robotic voice suggested, then tried my call again; only to end up with the same result. I decided I'd try to reach Shayla at her practice instead. Once again, my attempts were foiled when I got the same message in a different voice, letting me know the number was no longer in service. I soon began to wonder if Shayla's practice even existed. I decided there was only one way to find out. The Hughes Road Plaza sat in one of the highest traffic areas in the city of Madison and was one of the oldest structures. There were several business in the plaza including a small, retro boutique, but there was only one at the moment that interested me; the one that had Doctor Shayla E. Rice MD on the door. I strolled into the modestly decorated office then stepped up to the receptionist desk.

"May I help you?" The thin brunette asked from behind the counter.

"I would like to see Doctor Rice," I said. "My name is Octavia Whitmore."

"Do you have an appointment?" she asked, with bright eyes.

There is nothing worse than a dumb-ass question, I thought to myself. Hell, if I had an appointment wouldn't she be one of the first to know? After all she was the receptionist! I stared at her, took a deep breath then slowly exhaled. "No," I said smiling sweetly. "This is a personal visit. I'm a friend."

"One moment," she said. She advised me to have a seat then dialed a number on the phone sitting in front of her. I listened as she told the person on the other end that I was waiting. "Doctor Rice will be with you in just moment." she advised me.

"Thank you."

I sat down in one of the three leather chairs in the waiting room then directed my attention to the flat screen TV mounted on the wall. After several minutes the wooden door separating the waiting room from the rest of the office finally opened, and the doctor entered the waiting room.

"Octavia," she greeted me.

"Hello," I said smiling. "How are you?"

"I'm well," she said. "And yourself?"

"I'm good," I said, nodding my head. Silence. We looked at each other as if we were both stumped on where to go next with our conversation.

"Is there something I can help you with?" she asked.

"I'm waiting for Shayla," I advised her.

"I am Shayla."

"Doctor Shayla Rice," I clarified.

"I'm Doctor Rice," she advised me.

What the hell? I thought to myself. If I hadn't known any better I would have sworn I was having another attack, however, what I was seeing was clear and accurate. The woman standing next to me was tall and light skinned with auburn colored hair flowing down to her shoulder. She was clearly not the woman I was looking for.

*****

I entered the Ambiance with my bag swinging on one arm and the desire to get some clarification on my mind. I spotted Tabitha standing in the back of the restaurant near the kitchen speaking to my lead chef, Arthur. She wore cream-colored dress pants and a soft blue short-sleeve blouse and pointed heels. She seemed completely engulfed in her conversation, to the point where she didn't notice me walking up from behind her.

"Hello," I said, announcing my presence. Tabitha jumped slightly as she turned around facing me.

"Good to see you Octavia," Arthur said, smiling at me. Arthur held a single piece of paper in his hands and looked relieved to see me.

"Thank you Arthur," I said. "How is everything?" I looked from him to Tabitha, who was extremely quiet at the time.

"Everything is fine," Tabitha interjected. "Arthur and I were just discussing the game plan for today."

"Care to fill me in?" I asked, curious.

"We were going over the new items you selected to add to the menu," Arthur told me.

"What new items?" I asked, watching Tabitha.

"I thought it would be good to change things up," she said. "For instance a few kid's selections and—"

I raised my hand to let her know there was no need for her to continue.

"Arthur please disregard this," I said. "Our menu will remain as is until further notice. If I see a need to add on, I will do as I've always done in the past. I'll sit down with you and the rest of kitchen staff to discuss said changes." I could see Tabitha was once again pissed by my decision and I didn't give a damn.

"I got it," Arthur said. "Anything else?" He looked at me waiting for my response.

"Yes," I said. "I'd like to speak with you in the kitchen. Tabitha stay here." I followed Arthur in the kitchen then spoke to him and the other employees, many of which had been present during my altercation with Tamara. I apologized for my behavior and told them with confidence that it would never happen again. After finishing my conversation, I left the kitchen with a smile on my face and some of the weight lifted from my shoulder. Tabitha stood by the door waiting for me and undoubdtly eavesdropping.

"My office," I said, brushing past her. Inside my office I placed my handbag on my desk then walked around, easing down in my chair. Tabitha entered the room then shut the door.

"I was trying to surprise you," she said, sitting down on the other side of the desk. "I didn't—"

"What do you know about Shayla?" I asked, cutting her off. I stared at her gauging her reaction and waiting for her reply. She blinked then shrugged her shoulders.

"She's a doctor…"

"What else?"

"That's it," she said innocently. "Why? What's wrong?"

"Shayla Rice is a doctor, but she's not the woman that we met," I informed her. "I met the real Shayla Rice earlier today."

"What?" Tabitha asked. She looked just as surprised as I was when I found out. "Who do you think she is?"

"I don't have a clue," I said. "But I do plan on finding out."

"We definitely need to know," she said. "That's scary…"

"It is isn't it," I said. "That's why we can never be too safe."

"You're right," she said. "You never know a person's *real* intentions."

"That's true," I agreed. My phone chimed reminding me that I had an appointment scheduled with the security company. "You know Tabitha, Thursdays are some of our slowest days and we have plenty of coverage, why don't you take off and enjoy some sunshine today." I was expecting her to give me her usual spill about how we never know when the traffic might pick up and then put up a fight about leaving early. She didn't.

"I think I will take off," she said, standing. "I could use the rest."

"Wow, that was way too easy," I teased. "I was at least expecting a little fight."

"Not today," she said, "you win."

*****

I scanned my eyes over the invoice in front of me until I was content that there were no errors. I had spent an entire hour going over every invoice, receipt, and memo looking for discrepancies or inconsistencies in the reports I had been receiving at home and what the accounting system was showing at work. I had no fear that Tabitha or any of my other employees were stealing from me, but I also knew in business, life, and love… you can't be a damn fool. If your instinct is telling you something isn't right, then something isn't right. I knew that there was a whole lot of shit that wasn't right, I just hadn't figured it out at that moment. I was going over the bank deposit receipts when Heather and Kaitlyn knocked on the office door.

"Hey," they said in unison. Heather had only been on my staff for a few months, but she and Kaitlyn were already best friends. When we weren't busy, where you saw one, you saw the other. They laughed together and even finished each other's sentences, which is why I tried to keep them apart as much as possible because although they were both sweethearts, together they were annoying as hell.

"Hi there," I said, giving them my attention. "What's up?"

"Can we come in?"

"Sure." I smiled.

They stepped through the door both dressed in their uniform maroon pants and white button-front shirts.

"Okay, we would just like to say," Heather started, tucking her brunette strands behind her ear. "We have missed you soooooo much!" She fluttered her eyelashes dramatically.

"I told her we did," Kaitlyn said proudly.

"And we love our jobs," Heather continued.

"We really do," Kaitlyn agreed.

Silence

I could feel a "but" lingering in the air. I waited for them to continue and when neither one of them did, I asked, "But?"

"But it has been hell here ..." Kaitlyn answered.

"Total hell," Heather piped in.

"Without you," they said together.

"What's been going on?" I asked. I looked from one to the other observing the look in their brown eyes.

"Don't get us wrong, we like Tabitha, "Heather continued. "But she's…"

"…a bitch," Kaitlyn concluded. Heather looked at her with her eyebrows raised.

"Wait, can I say bitch?" Kaitlyn asked nervously.

"You just did," Heather and I said at the same time.

"You did that," Heather said. "But she is Octavia. She really is."

"She wasn't always like that," Kaitlyn explained, "When Amel was here she was mad cool."

"Super cool," Heather elaborated. "But lately she's bossy…"

"…rude…" Kaitlyn said smacking her lips.

"…and arrogant," Heather added. I knew what the two of them were saying was true. Tabitha had been swerving out her lane and getting out her place a lot lately with me. I could only imagine how she was interacting with the rest of my staff.

"And she blames everyone else for her screw ups," Kaitlyn advised me.

"Yeah," Heather said, rolling her eyes. "Even the day of the accident…" They looked at each other then back at me. "Can we talk about that?" Heather asked.

"Yes," I said.

"Okay, it was madness," Kaitlyn said. "Straight crazy! People were crying and there were reporters and police everywhere."

"We," she continued pointing at herself then at Heather. "Didn't know what to do and she—"

"She who?" I asked, confused.

"Tabitha," Heather advised me.

"She was nowhere to be found. She just up and disappeared!" Kaitlyn said, shrugging her shoulders. "But then when we later told her that Damon called…"

"And that he was mad," Heather added.

"Pissed!" Kaitlyn said dramatically. "Because no one called him to tell him what was happening…"

"But, I assumed, no we assumed, that Tabitha would have called him," Heather said. "I mean after all she was second in command as she *always* says."

I nodded my head while remaining quiet.

"But she didn't," Kaitlyn said dramatically. "Then she tried to get loud with us when we told her he called."

"See what we mean?" Heather asked. "She was supposed to be in charge and she dropped the ball but we got blamed."

"We loved Amel too, "Kaitlyn said. "But Tabitha was acting like she was the only who had the right to take a break." She rolled her eyes.

"It wasn't either of your faults," I said, speaking up. "It was just a lack of communication and it was difficult for every one that day." They both nodded their heads.

"But nonetheless, she was mad with us," Kaitlyn said.

"I'm sure Tabitha was just upset and took it out on the two of you," I suggested. "Which was wrong, but we all know everyone handles tragedies differently."

"You're right," Heather said. "We're just glad to get it off our chests."

"Relieved," Kaitlyn exhaled.

"The two of you can come to me anytime," I assured them. "And don't worry there are going to be some changes made now that I'm feeling better."

"Good," Heather smiled brightly.

"Perfect," Kaitlyn added.

"Good," I said. "Is there anything else the two of you would like to add?"

"That's it," they said smiling.

*****

It was just after three when Kharem, the technician with Stanley Security, arrived at my office. Kharem was a tall, handsome brother with dark skin and a physique that was proof that regular exercise does pay off. He looked to be in his late twenties and had a smiled that seemed to illuminate the room. After Kaitlyn escorted him to my office, I had to push her away to get her to go back to work.

"That'll be all," I said, slowly pushing the door closed in her face.

"Are you sure?" she asked from the other side of the door.

"Positive," I laughed. I watched Kharem as he positioned the small, wooden ladder he had brought with him against the wall, underneath the camera mounted in the corner of my office. I would be lying if I said that I paid no attention whatsoever to the way his khaki pants fit just right on his ass or that I failed to notice how the grey polo shirt with the name *Stanley Security* monogramed on the pocket, hugged the man's pecks to the point that it was almost erotic! I had noticed that and then some, and although I would never, ever touch…I was truly enjoying the show.

"I bet this is the problem," he said. I watched him as he did something to the back of the camera then slid the cell phone he had secured at his waist out of its cradle. I listened as he told the person on the other end to do a test, then told them, "Thanks" and put the phone back in the cradle.

"Done," he said, stepping down off the ladder.

"That was quick," I said.

"I know," he chuckled, while looking at me. "But it was an easy fix…the switch was off."

"You mean the power?"

"Yep," he answered. He closed the ladder then looked at me. "I called the center and they confirmed you're back online again."

"Thank you," I said. My focus was no longer on the man standing in front of me who was a fine example of God's craftsmanship. My focus was now on who had turned off the camera and what her reason was for doing so.

*****

I was in my own world for the rest of the afternoon as I sat in my office trying to process everything I had learned about or heard about Tabitha. The more I attempted to put the mix-matched pieces together, the more confused I became. I knew, without a shadow of a doubt, that she was the one who tampered with the camera in my office, but what I didn't know was why. All the money was adding up and there was nothing off about the books, but the more I thought about her behavior and actions, the more I began to think that not only was it good that I hadn't promoted her, but it was time for her to move on and explore other career opportunities.

When the fax came over with the drug and background test results for Joe, my thoughts and feelings about letting Tabitha go increased. I called Joe and made him an offer for the position, which he accepted, and then I advised him to come in Monday to fill out his paperwork. I had gathered my things together and gave Scar, my deejay, specific instructions on locking up when Heather knocked on the door and told me Tamara was on the phone. Apologizing to Tamara was one of the things I had put on my to do list, but I'll be honest, I had not made it a priority. It wasn't because I think Tamara deserved an explanation, but rather because I wasn't sure she would understand the explanation I had for her. After all, Damon didn't believe me at first, and if my husband, who knew me almost better than I knew myself, didn't believe me, I was sure Tamara was a lost cause.

"Hello," I answered.

"How are you?" she asked. I was expecting to hear anger and frankly hostility in her voice. However, her tone was quite pleasant.

"I'm good. Yourself?"

"Pretty good," she said.

Silence.

"I'm glad you called," I said. "Listen Tamara, I'm sorry about what happened. I wasn't myself…to be honest, I don't know who I was and at the moment I really didn't know who you were. I kinda blacked out.

"It's okay," she blew into the phone. "Well, it's not *okay*…but I understand you've been going through some things."

"That's putting it mildly," I said. "But thank you for understanding."

"Don't worry about it," she said. "Damon and I talked and he explained everything."

"I'm glad he did," I said. I felt relieved that Tamara wasn't looking for nor did I have to try and come up with any other explanations.

"So how are things with you?" I asked.

"Better," she said. "I'm settling in comfortably here and I'm beginning to think that this city may have exactly what I need."

"Huntsville is beautiful," I said. "I'm sure it's a lot slower than what you're accustomed to, but it's a great place to raise kids."

"I see that," Tamara said. "And that is something I'm definitely looking forward to someday... having my own son or daughter."

"There's nothing like them," I said thinking of Jasmine. "You'll lose sleep worrying about them, but you'll feel like the luckiest one in the world just by thinking about them."

"Well, hopefully soon, I'll be able to share those feelings," she said. "I'm very optimistic about that."

"It'll happen," I said. "Trust me."

"Well, I better let you go," she said. "I just wanted to call you and let you know there are no hard feelings."

"Thanks," I said, content with our conversation. "You take care."

"You too Octavia."

Chapter 18

Damon

When Octavia told me Tamara had called her, I got nervous instantly. After she shared the details of their conversation, I felt bad for second guessing Tamara's intentions. Octavia told me about Shayla and what had taken place when she went to what she thought was her office; my natural instincts and desire to protect my family took over. I wanted to know who the woman really was, and like my wife, I needed an explanation of why she had chosen to lie. I didn't take Shayla or whomever she was as a threat, if she wanted to harm Octavia she had already had the opportunity. For this reason, I felt my investigation could wait until after the weekend.

Tabitha called out, which meant Octavia was short staffed for the morning shift, so like the true leader she is, she went in to cover the floor until her lead hostess at the Ambiance 2 was available to cover Tabitha's shift at the Ambiance. I sat reclining by our pool watching as Octavia held on to Jasmine, while she splashed and kicked playfully in the pool. I don't know what Amel's mother said to my love when the two of them had their conversation that day, but whatever it was, it had been a lifesaver. Octavia was once again the vibrant and consistently loving woman I married, and the two of us were once again communicating properly. I stood then grabbed one of the plush bath towels sitting on the table next to me. Octavia lifted Jazz up and out of the water, then put her on the patio. I stooped down, holding one of the towels open for my daughter as she walked, dripping wet in my direction. She wore a pink one-piece *Disney Princess* bathing suit and hot pink plastic floatation devices around each of her arms.

"Daddy did you see me?" she asked, while I patted her skin dry.

"Yes baby," I smiled. "Daddy saw you. Good job baby girl." I removed the floaters from each of her arms, then helped her slip her feet into her matching pink flip flops. She smiled, then kissed my nose. I secured the towel around her body, then instructed her to go inside and wait in the kitchen. I directed my attention to my other baby who had just gotten out of the pool. She wore a shimmering gold two piece that left very little to my imagination.

"Did you see me Daddy?" Octavia asked, seductively. I grabbed the second towel then held it open allowing her to walk inside my embrace.

"You know I did," I said, licking my lips. I leaned down, then kissed her lightly on the forehead.

"I saw you too," she said. "Looking like a king guarding his throne."

"This is what I do," I said. She reached down in between us, grabbing and squeezing my dick through my shorts and causing my man to jump.

"I'll show you what I can do later," she said suggestively. "But then you are already familiar with what I'm capable of."

"Ain't nothing like a reminder," I said quickly. "You can give me two or three reminders if you want."

"I bet I can," she laughed then gave me a peck on the lips. "I'm going to go shower and give Jazz a bath. I shall return."

"Hurry back," I told her.

*****

For lunch I prepared the three of us turkey subs and pasta salad; then spread a large blanket on the lawn and treated my wife and daughter to a family picnic.

"So you're sure that's what you want to do?" I asked, looking at Octavia. She had just told me that she was planning on letting Tabitha go. I personally felt it was an excellent choice, but I chose not to give my unsolicited opinion at the moment.

"Positive," she said. "There's just too much I'm feeling right now and it's not a good feeling."

"Then you have to do what's best babe," I said. "Follow your first instinct." I watched my daughter as she took a long gulp form her sippy cup. "Eat your sandwich first," I told her. She nodded her head, took a bite of the sandwich sitting in front of her, then picked up her cup again. Octavia laughed then eased the cup out of Jasmine's hands. She continued to express her feeling of optimism about her new hire Joe when her words were halted by Jasmine making a strange gasping noise. We looked at our daughter simultaneously as her eyes rolled back in her head right before she fell back against the grass, and began shaking violently.

Chapter 19

Octavia

I squeezed Damon's hand until my own fingers were numb as the two of us waited, along with my parents, in the emergency room of Crestwood Hospital. The seizure Jasmine experienced had lasted less than a minute, but it was the longest seconds of my life. Damon and I dialed 911 then met the ambulance they dispatched on the way to the hospital. The physician on duty asked me and Damon a series of questions from what Jasmine was eating to what products we used in our home. Now, an hour and a half later, we were waiting for the results of the blood work and scans they performed, so that they could determine what caused the episode before we could take our daughter home.

I was just about ready to demand an update on my daughter's condition when I spotted a thin, dark-skinned woman dressed in a plain blue skirt and blouse approaching.

The woman was accompanied by a uniformed officer from the Huntsville Police Department. Damon dropped my hand and immediately stood facing the woman. I followed my husband's lead and also stood, along with my mother and father.

"Mr. and Mrs. Whitmore, my name is Cynthia Keys, I'm a case worker with Child Protective Services," she said.

"What?" I asked, looking around at my family. I knew whenever CPS was contacted, there were signs or symptoms of abuse or neglect. My daughter was far from being a victim of either of the two.

"What can we do for you Cynthia?" Damon asked calmly.

"I'd like to speak to you in private," she stated, looking at my parents.

"Anything you'd like to say to me and my wife, you can say in front of her parents," Damon stated. The woman took a deep breath then exhaled.

"Very well," she said. "Mr. and Mrs. Whitmore, the reason I'm here is because there were traces of drugs in your daughter's system."

"What kind of drugs?" I asked.

"What kind has she been exposed to?" Cynthia asked accusingly.

"Excuse me!" I asked, raising my voice.

"I'm asking what your daughter has been exposed to," she said staring at me.

"If you're asking if I, or my wife, use drugs, "Damon

said, "the answer is no."

"Who else has she been around?" the woman asked, looking at my parents.

"You wait just a damn minute," Mama snapped. She looked ready to beat the woman's ass and I was ready and willing to help her.

"Charlene," Daddy said, putting his hand on her shoulder. "I want you and baby girl to give Damon and myself a moment alone with Ms. Keys and this nice officer." I looked at Daddy like he had lost his mind.

Hell no! I thought. I looked at Mama, she co-signed with her eyes.

"It's okay Octavia," Damon said, stroking my back with his fingertips. "This will only take a few minutes."

"I don't know about that," Cynthia said sarcastically. I cut my eyes at her, giving her a glare of death.

"Like I said," Damon said firmly, "this will only take a few minutes." I looked at my husband and saw a seriousness that made me afraid. I looked at my father and saw a seemingly familiar stare.

"Come on Mama," I said. "Let's go for a walk." My mother cut her eyes at Cynthia one last time before following behind me. The two of us walked out the emergency room exit into the parking lot. The sun had set, casting a kaleidoscope of burnt orange and red across the sky.

"This right here is why people sue their asses," Mama began to vent. "They don't know what or why, so the first thing they want to do is scream abuse or neglect."

I nodded my head in agreement. I listened as Mama continued to rant until I spotted Doctor Aurora across the parking lot. He was standing by the driver's side door of a black Ferrari with the initials, VTT on the licenses plate. He stood with one hand on the car and the other in his pants pocket. I watched him as he made dramatic gestures with his hands. It was obvious he, and whomever he was speaking to, were having a serious conversation and from what I could see in his body language, a heated discussion.

I heard the automatic doors of the ER open, and I felt my heart skip a beat when I saw Damon exiting through the door carrying Jasmine in his arms. Our daughter looked like nothing had ever happened. She was smiling while holding onto her Daddy's neck. She carried a small, white stuffed bear in her hands that had something written all over it. I cried as I rushed up to my husband and daughter.

Chapter 20

Damon

I hadn't had contact with Detective Jennings since I discovered he was also playing nice with Gator; one, because I had no respect for a man without loyalty; and two, because I had been following all the laws of the land, keeping my hands clean, and therefore I had no use for the man. However, I now needed him to call in a favor and I was willing to pay him well for it. I made the call, and magically within ten minutes Cynthia was told to fallback. I could see the disappointment in the woman's eyes as she advised me there had been a mistake. I could hear the defeat in her voice as she advised the doctor that performed my daughter's tests and her checkup, that I was free to take my baby girl home with me. The truth is even if Jennings hadn't jumped on my bandwagon, there was no way in hell I, nor Charles was going to allow Jasmine to go into foster care. Cynthia would have died attempting to accomplish the task, I would have made sure of that.

I had managed to get Jasmine released to me and Octavia, but when I spoke with the on-call doctor and saw Jasmine's test results with my own eyes, I knew that was only half of my battle. The other half was finding the person responsible for giving drugs to my child.

"The drug is called Mescaline," I explained to Octavia. The two of us sat with her parents in our dining room, discussing the information the doctor had provided to me and Charles. Jasmine lay tucked in on the sofa, next door in our family room.

"What is that?" Octavia asked.

"It's a psychedelic drug," Charles told her. "It can cause hallucinations, make you think you're having out of body experiences…things of that nature."

"But Jazz had a seizure," Octavia said.

"The truth is every one reacts differently." Charles answered. "She's a child. Most studies conducted report the effects these drugs have on adults not children."

"I still think they got it wrong," Charlene said. "Maybe Jazz had an allergic reaction to something."

"The only thing she did different today was swim and we had a picnic," I told Charles. "We were eating when she had the seizure." I was trying to come up with a sensible explanation, but I kept coming up empty handed. Jasmine had eaten the same thing as me and Octavia, if her food was laced with the drug, then mine and Octavia's would have been too.

"What did she have to drink?" Charlene inquired.

"Juice," Octavia replied.

"Actually it was tea," I corrected her. "I made a pitcher earlier. Octavia's favorite." Charles and I went back and forth with a suggestion here and there from Charlene. Octavia, on the other hand was extremely quiet. I watched Octavia as she typed on her cellphone while staring at the screen.

"What are you doing bae?" I asked curiously.

"Google," she said. She was quiet for several minutes as she read from her phone. "Son of a b…" She mumbled, before pushing away from the table then marching out the room.

"Octavia," I called. "What's wrong?" I looked around the table at her parents, hoping and praying she was not having another episode. Octavia returned to the dining room a minute later carrying a bag of tea leaves, she dropped the bag on the table.

"What's up baby girl?" Charles asked, examining the bag.

"It's in the tea," Octavia said angrily. "She put it in the tea."

*****

Charles said it would take approximately twenty-four hours for his friends at the police lab to confirm the contents mixed with the tea leaves. I didn't need a confirmation. The story Octavia told us of her hallucinations and the time frame was consistent with the time frame she received the gift from Tabitha. What I didn't understand was what had taken place at the Ambiance.

"The day I had the first panic attack, Tabitha brought me coffee," Octavia explained. "The day you, me, and Tamara had lunch, Tabitha brought out our food."

"She did, but we had the same thing." I reminded her.

"But then I ordered a tea," she said. "Before then, I was the only person that had water."

"She did all this because she's mad about not getting a promotion?" Charles asked angrily.

"I think it's deeper than that Daddy," Octavia explained. "When I talked to Amel's mom she said that the autopsy report showed LSD in Amel's blood stream."

"You think she drugged Amel? Charlene asked, shaking her head.

"I do," Octavia replied.

"Why?" Daddy asked.

"I don't know," Octavia said. "But Ms. Fletcher said that a man came to see her the day before Amel died. He wore a suit and expensive shoes." I looked at Charles wondering if he was thinking of the same person I was thinking of; Gator.

"Gator was the first person to came to mind," Octavia continued. "But that would be impossible."

"Maybe Amel was involved with some other dealers," Charles suggested.

"There's a link we're missing," I said. "I just don't know who or what, but I'm going to find out now. I'm going to pay Tabitha a visit."

"Not without me you're not," Octavia said.

"Neither one of you are going to do anything," Charlene said. "Our family has been through too much for the two of you to be putting yourselves in danger. Charles is going to get the tea to the lab, then once we have confirmation, we'll let the authorities handle it. Does everyone understand?" I looked at Charles. He nodded his head.

"Charlene's right," I said, looking at Octavia. "Let's just sit back and see what happens." Octavia shot her eyes in my direction. I told her to trust me, using only my eyes.

"Fine," she said defeated. "Understood."

"Why don't the two of you let Jazz come home with us tonight?" Charles suggested. "Give you some alone time to process all that's happened."

"That's something I agree with," Charlene said.

I nodded my head in agreement, while silently thinking to myself that this would be one time I would let my mother-in-law down. Tabitha's antics could have cost my daughter and my wife their lives. I didn't have time to wait for the authorities to handle it, I needed my answer and a resolution immediately.

Ten minutes later, while I changed into jeans and a t-shirt, I listened to Octavia rant and rave on how selfish I was being for wanting to confront Tabitha alone.

"Charlene is right," I told her. "It's too dangerous. We don't know who she's involved with and I'd rather not take any chances with you."

"We've been taking chances since we met," she said, "It's what we do."

"Not tonight," I told her. "Tonight I go it alone." I could tell she wanted to protest but she didn't; instead, she rolled her eyes while shaking her head at me. "Can you just trust me on this?" I questioned. "Respect my wishes? Please baby?"

"I'll go pull her address up for you?" she exhaled. "I have it saved on my database down in the office."

"Thanks bae," I said. I gave her a warm hug, then a quick peck on the lips. "I love you."

"I love you too," she said, pulling away. I knew Octavia was disappointed, but there was no way I was going to risk her life. I sat down on the edge of the bed admiring her from behind as she exited the bedroom. I slipped my feet in my sneakers then retrieved the 45mm I kept hidden in our closet and secured it in the waistband of my pants. I stepped down the staircase and found a note waiting for me at the landing of the stairs.

"I got this. I love you. Octavia"

"Damnit!" I screamed aloud, before grabbing my keys and walking out the door.

Chapter 21

Octavia

There was no way Damon was going to leave me behind while he addressed Tabitha about me and Amel. I loved my hubby's protective nature, but there are some things a woman must do for herself. I reminded myself of this as I pulled up into the gated community where Tabitha lived. I had stored Tabitha's address inside my phone and had the building and unit number memorized by the time I arrived. I grabbed my hand bag, preparing to exit my car, but halted my stride when I saw a figure coming out of the darkness under the street light. I waited until I had a clear view and that's when I realized it was Doctor Aurora coming down the sidewalk leaving from building 5000; the building where Tabitha lived. I climbed back behind the wheel of my car while observing the doctor's every move. I watched him until he walked up, unlocking the door to a red Porsche, climbed in, then sped off. I decided Tabitha could wait. I needed to catch up with the doctor. I revived my engine, then followed in the direction he left.

"Where are you?" Damon answered on the first ring.

"I was sitting in the parking lot of Tabitha's complex," I told him. "Until I saw Doctor Aurora coming from her building."

"First of all, you were dead wrong for that stunt you pulled," he said. "Second, why would he be visiting Tabitha?"

"That's what I want to know," I said.

"He may be the missing link," Damon concluded. "And our drug supplier."

"I think you're right," I agreed. I could see the Porsche two cars in front of me. He was headed west outside the city limits.

"Okay, so I'll find out what's up with the doc," Damon advised me. "I still want to pay Tabitha a visit, but that can wait. How much longer do you have until you're home?"

"Um, about forty minutes," I said lightly.

"Octavia where are you going?"

"I'm trailing the doctor right now, "I said, bracing myself for Damon's outrage.

"Octavia turn around and come home now!" He demanded. "It's not safe…" I listened as Damon went on and on about my being reckless and putting my life in danger and how he wanted me to go home immediately.

"Do you understand?" he asked, breathing heavily into the phone.

"Yes," I said. "I love you too." I hung up before he could say anything else. The car I was trailing exited off the main highway onto the service road leading further into rural Madison County. I eased off the accelerator allowing my speed to decrease and to put some additional space between the two of us. There were houses along the road, but no street lights and an abundance of winding, deadly curves. The road finally became straight again; leaving room for cars to pull over and out of the way of traffic, but the number of homes close together slowly began to decrease.

Doctor Aurora pulled off the main road onto a long driveway. I stayed on the main road driving slowly pass the drive then coming to a complete stop approximately a half of a mile from the entrance. I pulled over to the edge of the street then turned off my headlights. I waited...peeping out the window for signs of movement from the doctor. I saw the interior dome light come on in the car as the doctor stepped out. There were lights coming from the inside of the home, but the outside was completely dark, covered and shaded by the surrounding trees and the night sky. Once I saw light spilling out the front door, I knew the man who held my interest had gone inside.

The sound of my phone ringing caused me to jump and further troubled my already shaken nerves. I placed my phone on vibrate, allowing my husband to go to voicemail. I grabbed my purse, securing the strap across my body, turned the interior light off inside my vehicle and climbed out with my keys in hand. I stepped onto the paved driveway being cautious and careful of staying close to the large weeping willows aligning my path. As I stepped slowly, moving closer to the home, I quietly wished I had chosen sneakers rather than my ensemble of open-toed sandals and my above the knee—off the shoulder—eyelet dress.

When I got close enough so that the home was in clear view, I saw that the house was two-stories with a long wooden porch that stretched the length of the front of the house. In front of the home, Doctor Aurora's car was parked next to the Ferrari I saw him standing next to at the ER, and a dark-colored SUV. It was in that moment that I came to the realization that I didn't have a clue or a plan of what I should do next. In my mind, a little voice I'd like to refer to as common sense, was telling me to haul my ass back to my car and get home. However, there was something, probably my sick-curiosity, pulling me closer. I chose to listen to the latter of the two.

I started to move in closer towards a window facing the west side of the property when the door opened, I quickly ducked behind a tree easing down in the damp grass. My heart was beating so loud I was certain whomever was coming out would discover me.

Get it together Octavia, I told myself. *Sweet Baby Jesus, if you get me out of this alive, I promise I will never be this stupid again!* I prayed. I was hoping I hadn't recited that prayer previously when I was caught in an awkward position, but knowing me; I had!

I heard the doctor talking, along with the voice of a woman. I couldn't make out what they were saying, and finally I heard the door shut and later the sound of an engine starting. I held my breath as light from the headlights of the car were cast over the property surrounding me and finally, I heard the car moving down the driveway. I was scared as hell to look, but I did anyway and I saw the red glare of the taillights as the vehicle pulled out the driveway, making a left, and turning onto the main road. I sat in my position waiting to see if the car might come back or if someone else may exit the house.

When I felt the coast was clear, I eased back up, standing straight, then tipped toed over to the window. I peeked inside the window scanning my eyes across the room. The living room was exceptionally decorated with dark furnishings and glass. From my position at the window, I could see a glimpse of what looked like the kitchen and a shadow moving around the room. I could also see another window. I stepped slowly along the side of the home hoping the other window would give me a better view of whomever was inside.

The full moon gracing the sky illuminated the back side of the home with just the right amount of light, to allow me to see where I was going. I cautiously stepped on to the air conditioning unit, so that I could reach the higher window. The woman in the kitchen moved back and forth across the floor, dancing while clutching her arms close to her breast. She had her back to me as she spun around and around on her heels. The skirt of the white dress she wore swayed and flowed with her movements like water flowing through a calm stream. She spun around facing the window and giving a clear view of her face and her body.

"Shayla!" I whispered.

I removed my phone from my bag only to discover I had no service. I wanted to call Damon and let him know I had found the woman we had so many questions about, but my call would have to wait until I reached my car. I watched Shayla as she hurried out the kitchen towards the stairs. I jumped down off my perch landing on the ground below. I eased along the side of the house staring at the screen of my phone. As I came past the side of the house, I was stopped in my tracks when Shayla stepped in front of me.

"Hello Octavia," she said politely. "I've been expecting you. Why don't you join me inside?"

"You know you look really busy," I said lightly. "It's probably best if I come back later." I heard a light click as the moonlight bounced off the chrome nose of the gun she held in her hand. I looked down at the weapon, then back up at the woman.

"Or now is as good a time as any," I said.

She snatched my phone from my hands then pushed me in the direction of the house. Inside Shayla ordered me to sit down on the sofa. My cell phone let off a light chirp indicating I once again had service; followed by several additional tones notifying me I had a voicemail message and text. It was clear that I was back in service, however, as I stared at Shayla's weapon, it was clear that said service was just a little too late.

Ain't that some shit! I thought to myself. *America's most reliable my ass!*

"Who knows you're here?" Shayla asked watching me.

"No one," I said honestly. She looked at me then shook her head.

"Call Damon," she said, extending the phone to me. "Tell him you're okay."

"I'll pass. If you're going to kill me," I said, staring her in the eyes, "just get it over with." I was afraid hearing my husband's voice would evoke tears and quite possibly fear in me; not the fear of dying, but the fear of never seeing him or our daughter again. Despite my circumstances, I was extremely calm. I guess my feelings of peace derived from the fact that it wasn't the first time I had been on the other end of a gun, and I knew that whenever my time on earth was up, there would be nothing that could be done and fear would be a useless emotion. Maybe in some scary way, all the death and mayhem I had seen and experienced had made me numb.

"If you don't call, I will," Shayla said coldly. "Then when he gets here, because you and I both know he'll come" she paused for a moment before continuing, "I'll make sure he's dead before his feet hit the ground."

I snatched the phone from her hand and dialed my husband's number. When our conversation was over I told him I loved him then handed Shayla the phone. She grabbed the phone then tossed it on the leather chair adjacent to the sofa where I was sitting.

"Octavia, what do you know about karma?" she asked. I looked at her confused about where she was headed with our conversation.

"I know what you put out is what you receive," I said playing along.

"Yes," she said. "What goes around comes around." I looked at her curious as to if she realized that karma also applied to her.

"Where are you going with this?" I asked impatiently. She looked slightly offended that I was ruining her moment.

"Patience," she said coldly. "You'll be dead soon enough."

"Who are you?" I questioned. "And why are you doing this?" She walked over to the chair then eased down sitting on the edge.

"My name is Venetta," she said. "Venetta Bailey."

I thought real hard trying to remember where I had heard her name before. She looked at me with low, dark eyes.

"You don't even have a clue?" she asked. "Do you?"

"I've heard of you from somewhere," I said, still processing my thoughts. "I just can't put my finger on it."

"Maybe you're more familiar with my family name," she said, "Douglass."

I remembered in an instant where I had heard of her."

"You're Gator's sister.

"Yes," she said proudly. "I prefer to call him Leon, I'm not big on nicknames."

"But you're big on making up a whole identity," I said frowning. "Wow…"

She cocked her head to the side while looking at me.

"I didn't make up Shayla's identity," she remind me, "she's very real. I'm just not her."

"Why?" I asked.

"Everyone deals with pain and loss differently," she said. "When my son died, my husband Terrance dealt with the pain by declaring war and seeking revenge on the ones responsible."

I remembered all too clearly how Terrance handled their son's death; by helping hold me captive, plotting to murder Damon, and blowing Lena's brains out. The man flipped completely out! He was the poster child for therapy.

"I tried to cope by being a better person and trying to keep my focus on the positive." I remained silent. "But you know where that thinking got me?" she asked. "It got me to bury my husband less than eight months after I buried my child. It lead to my brother, who was my best friend, going to prison for life. All the family and support that I knew and loved instantly diminished to shit, and the bitch who claimed she would always be there for him and always be my sister, ran off with his attorney!" She took a quick breath then continued. "So all that positive bullshit went down the toilet and I decided my husband was right...sometimes the best way to mourn is through revenge."

"I'm not responsible for what happened to your family," I said calmly. "I was a victim in the whole mess."

"You were," she agreed. "But my husband would still be alive, and my brother would be free if Leon had just killed you when he had the chance. "

"Why didn't he?" I asked.

"Our mother was murdered," she informed me. "When Leon established his organization he made a pledgethat he would never make another child suffer the pain that we experienced growing up without our mother...that's why."

I would have found Gator's code honorable, but he had probably ordered the hit on hundreds of men. So, children don't need fathers? Gator was twisted and crazy as hell; there is nothing noble about that.

"So, I saw an opportunity," she continued. "Infiltrate your team like you did ours. Slip into your business and see if I could recoup some of my losses, if only financially." She crossed her legs then reclined in the chair. "I reached out to Amel and made her a proposition; if she could get me inside your business I would give her a free pass... her life. However, she was quite adamant about not betraying you, even after I sent a friend of mine to visit her mother in Selma."

"Get to the part when you decided to kill her," I said.

"That came when I found another one of your little peons who was willing to assist..."

"Tabitha," I concluded.

"No," she frowned. "Kaitlyn."

Kaitlyn? I thought.

"Yes, Kaitlyn," she said, reading my mind. I listened as Venetta described in detail that Kaitlyn had been the one who drugged Amel and myself while making it appear as Tabitha was involved. She had been the one who turned off the camera and even pretended to be Tanitha when the security company called.

"Tabitha was an innocent bystander," Venetta continued.

"What do you mean *was?*"

"She's dead now. But that's only due to the fact that she learned a little too much and was planning on exposing me." she explained. "So, I had Aurora take care of her." I felt the wells of my eyes filling with tears.

"You killed her?" I asked.

"Don't worry," she said. "We gave her a little something that will help her sleep permanently. But it was completely painless."

I couldn't believe the woman's complete disregard for life. The more I looked at her the angrier I became.

"So we had our game plan and our players," she continued. "Amel was to come in sick and once you arrived I would take care of \you—do what my brother should have done long ago. However, we had an interesting turn of events that evening."

"When Amel killed herself," I said.

"That too," she said. "But no, the ultimate turn came when you entered the office and I saw you were pregnant." She smiled brightly. "You were positively radiant. So I decided to let you live a little longer. Well, as karma would have it...you went into labor." She paused then laughed. "As if shit couldn't get more interesting or better for me!"

She looked genuinely thrilled as she reminisced. I listened as she went into detail, filling in the blanks of what I had been missing. Venetta explained when she came to my assistance in the middle of the road she knew everyone would be distracted and caught up in the chaos, which was her perfect time to drug me. I remembered the pain in my arm.

"I got you to the hospital in record time," she said. "And I made sure you had the best care money could buy." I knew she was referring to Doctor Aurora. "However, when I left the plan was that you would be dead. So simple, but you made it." She stood, then walked over to the sofa. "Quite naturally, I knew I had to finish the job—"

"So you came back later that night," I concluded. "But Damon was with me."

"Bingo," she grinned. "Needless to say when Aurora advised me you didn't remember and we were safe, I decided simply to count my blessings and let bygones be bygones. I believe in giving second chances. But now we're here and it's clear I should have followed my first instinct…" She rose from her chair then walked over to me. "Let's go," she said grabbing my arm and pulling me up from the couch. Venetta pulled me close, holding on to my arm with one hand and poking the nose of the gun against my ribs with the other. "Another thing I believe in is wrapping up all loose ends." She continued. "Saying the proper goodbyes. I didn't get that with my son or my husband, but I'm going to show you that despite everything, I truly have a good heart."

"That's all a matter of opinion," I said dryly.

"Now is not the time to be cute," she said. As we made it to the top of the stairs, I could hear sounds of music playing. "Go," she said, shoving me in the back. "Third door on the right."

I hesitated briefly then walked up to the closed door. I turned the handle then pushed the door open and stepped inside. The room was simply painted with white walls and all white baby furniture. There was crib, changing table, and a large rocking chair.

"You see Octavia, I lost my son, but when I met you the winds of fate shifted giving me another opportunity."

"What do you mean?" I asked, fearful of what she may say next. She pushed me forward, nudging me towards the crib. I stepped forward until I was able to see the baby boy sleeping peacefully.

"Beautiful isn't he?" Venetta asked. "You and Damon did good."

I shot my eyes at her confirming that I heard her correctly. She nodded her head.

"Josiah..." I whispered. I felt an overflowing of hope inside of me as I came to terms with the fact that my son was alive.

Chapter 22

Damon

I was en route towards Tabitha's apartment when I spoke to Octavia and she advised me that she was trailing Doctor Aurora. I immediately contacted her father to let him know what was going on. Charles was in the process of having Octavia's phone tracked when she finally called me to let me know she was fine and going by the Ambiance before returning home. I couldn't trust my wife to do only what she had planned and I knew from experience that she would switch it up then contact me afterwards. I decided it was in both of our best interest for me to keep her company while at the restaurant until she was ready to go home. At night the mood at the Ambiance was little more laid back. There was still the same great service and food, but the crowd was more casually dressed and the normal jazz music selection was replaced with R&B and a little

Hip Hop. The hostess on duty advised me that Octavia had not arrived yet. I decided rather than waiting in her office I would sit upstairs in the lounge and have a drink.

Although, Octavia was doing one hundred percent better, I had yet to allow alcohol back in our home. I sat at a small table by the railing overlooking the dining room below while sipping on the ice-cold *Heineken* in front of me. When I saw the doors leading to the front entrance open, I instantly shot a glance in that direction. I was looking for my wife, but instead spotted someone else that interested me. I watched as Kaitlyn came up then greeted the man with open arms.

What the fuck? I said aloud.

I dropped a five dollar bill on the table then casually headed downstairs to the dining room. I stood at the bottom of the stairs watching as the two of them disappeared behind the wall leading to Octavia's office. A minute later, the door opened and I glanced around making sure no one was watching me then followed them. I stood outside the office leaning against the door. The music flowing through the restaurant speakers made it impossible for me to hear what the two of them were saying. I decided it was time to get up close and personal. I knocked on the office door then waited.

"Yes…" The smile in Kaitlin's eyes quickly turned to fear at the sight of me. She stepped back slowly moving away from the door. Doctor Aurora sat on the sofa reclining comfortably. He sat up abruptly when he saw me. I pulled the door closed then locked it.

"Sit down." I instructed Kaitlyn. "I want to know what's going on," I said. "And I want to know right now." I waited for them to respond and when neither of them did, I decided to provide them with a little motivation. I reached behind me, removing the piece I had secured in the waistband of my pants.

The color faded from Kaitlin's face as she looked from me to the doctor then back to me. I could tell she was ready to crack already and tell me everything, the doctor on the other hand remained calm and didn't as much as blink. It was clear the man had been through this or something similar before. "Why don't you go first," I said to Kaitlyn. She looked too afraid to even open her mouth to speak. I cocked the gun to see if I could further motivate her. It worked. In less than sixty seconds Kaitlyn gave me complete details of how she helped Gator's sister, Venetta, with her plot to ruin my wife.

"Why would she want to hurt Tabitha?" I questioned looking at Kaitlyn.

"She didn't," she said lowly. "I did. I hated her. She was a royal bitch!"

"Do you know what your actions have caused?" I asked. "You've hurt good people for no reason and my daughter could have died from ingesting that bull shit."

She lowered her eyes. "Sorry," she said.

I looked at her like she had lost her damn mind. All the *sorries* in the world couldn't make what Kaitlyn had done alright.

"What role did you play doc?" I asked, looking at the man. He kept a straight face and his mouth tight while looking at me. The doctor obviously did not know the severity of the situation. If he did he would have taken Kaitlin's lead. I wasn't in the mood to repeat myself. I marched up to the sofa grabbing him my shirt and pushing the nose of the gun against his forehead. Kaitlyn began to cry louder.

"Shut up!" I yelled, cutting my eyes at her. Her face was completely red and her hands shook as she covered her own mouth with them.

"You have exactly one minute to tell me what I want to know," I said, staring him in his eyes. "Or I will without hesitation paint the walls with your brains."

"I've been the physician for the Douglass family for eight years," he started. "My father was inducted to their family and after he took his own life that debt became mine. Some of my colleagues think I have a long list of white collar clients. The truth is there is no one on my client list who's name doesn't end with Douglass, who doesn't work for them, or who they haven't sent to me."

"So you were hired to treat my wife?" I asked, releasing my grip on him. I stepped back giving the man room to breathe and lowering my gun.

"Yes," he said. "Venetta called me on her way to the emergency room and demanded that I be present," he exhaled. "She had already administered Octavia a chloroform injection to sedate her. However, Chloroform is extremely toxic and has been known to cause many health concerns including cardiac arrhythmia. Arrhythmia can cause strokes."

The details of the puzzle were all coming together and starting to form the perfect psychotic picture. "That injection caused her heart to stop and the stroke." I stated, fuming. I stepped back from the sofa.

"I'm sure if it had not been for the drug," he said. "Your wife would have had a normal delivery."

"Is that what happened to my son?" I questioned. *Silence.* I paced back and forth across the office floor as the doctor rambled on about how he saved Octavia.

"That's why I induced the coma to try and prevent any physical damage...and it worked...it worked! I wanted her to live Damon. I did. Venetta wanted her dead, but I saved her!"

I cut my glare at Kaitlyn, heated from her participation in the pain that was inflicted upon my family. She too deserved to die right along with the good doctor. The image of Gator and the torment he had put my wife through filled my head; causing me to feel no regard for the lives of neither the man, nor the woman before me, and giving me less of a reason to spare either of them.

"On your knees," I ordered, standing still.

"No...no...don't do this," the man pleaded. "Please!"

I grabbed his shirt pulling him up from the sofa then pushed him to the floor. He began to recite something that sounded like a prayer in his native tongue. Kaitlyn looked horrified as she looked from the doctor to me.

"You too!" I ordered.

"Noooo," she begged, shaking her head.

"Now!" I ordered, ignoring the desperation and fear etched in her face. She eased from her position on the sofa then sat on her knees, shaking like wind-threatened leaves on a tree.

"I saved her..." Aurora cried. "I did...I did..."

I tuned out the man's cries then extended my arm, pressing the gun to the side of his head.

"No, I can help you...I can help..." He pleaded.

"There is nothing you can do for me," I grunted through clenched teeth. "You two have done enough."

"No...no!" Aurora flinched as he raised his head. The color in his face had faded. He now bore the paint of fear, the anguish of anticipation that one displays when they know all hope is gone. "Please...I can..." he said. "I...can...help...I can...I...I...can help you get your son."

Chapter 23

Octavia

"He's going to be a heartbreaker isn't he?" Venetta asked, standing behind me.

I ignored her remark while lifting my sleeping baby boy up into my arms. I knew the moment I saw his full-brown cheeks and pudgy nose that Venetta was telling the truth. He was my son. I felt a knot rising in my throat as tears stood on the edge of my eyelids. I lowered my head, pressing my lips against his warm forehead.

"Why?" I asked lowly.

"It was fate," Venetta said. "I lost the loves of my life, but miraculously I was put in a position where I could know that kind of love again. I wanted to destroy you, but the truth is without you, I wouldn't have my son. I think it's necessary for me to say, thank you!"

I turned around looking at her. She had a smile of happiness and contentment on her face. "Can I have a moment alone with him?" I asked, turning my back to her. "Please?"

"I normally wouldn't recommend it," she said. "But I'm in a good mood. Just make it quick. And if you can, try not to wake him up. He's a really good baby, but I don't like disturbing his rest, he gets super cranky."

I bit my lower lip to suppress my urge to reply. Once I heard the bedroom door close, I kissed my son then laid him back in the crib.

"Mommy will be back," I whispered. I dried my eyes with the back of my hands. Venetta's first mistake was taking my son; her second was letting me know that my son was alive. It now made sense why I felt so detached from the baby in the morgue, he wasn't mine and instead some random corpse Doctor Aoura had provided. I had been feeling like something was reaching out to me. I now knew that force was my son.

"Venetta!" I screamed. "Something's wrong with the baby!" Josiah jumped awakened from his sleep and began to cry loudly. The door to the bedroom flew open as Venetta came rushing into the room.

"What is it?" she demanded. I pulled my fist back then delivered a solid punch that landed to her jaw before quickly hitting her with another one. She lost her balance and dropped the gun. I raised my leg, landing a kick to the side of her rib cage. Venetta crawled on the floor towards the spot where the gun had fallen, but she was too late. I punched her in the back of her head, throwing her off course. I grabbed the piece then stepped back while aiming it at her. I stepped backwards moving toward the crib while keeping my eyes glued on my enemy.

"Shhh," I said. I reached down in the crib then picked up Josiah. "It's okay." I cradled my son in my arm while keeping an eye and the gun aimed at Venetta.

"You're not taking my son," she mumbled.

"You're right," I said. "I'm taking mine." I stepped past her with my finger on the trigger ready to pull it at any moment. Downstairs, I grabbed my phone and keys and had one hand on the door when I heard a clap, then felt a stinging sensation in my left arm. Venetta stood on the stairs holding a small black pistol. I looked at my arm and saw that she had only grazed it, but that did not stop it from hurting like hell.

"Put him down," she ordered. "Or the next one will be through your head!" I held Josiah tightly, clutching his warm body to my chest.

"No," I said backing away.

"Give me my son—" The front door swung open, interrupting her vent. I watched as my husband charged Venetta, slamming her against the staircase banister. I watched as Damon drove his fist into her face, causing her head to sway back and forth like a rag doll. Venetta lay on the floor with blood dripping from her mouth. I watched as Damon grabbed the pistol Venetta used to graze me then aimed it at the woman. I could practically feel his anger flowing throughout the room.

"Damon," I said. He looked up as if he had heard

a ghost then stared into my eyes. "No," I said. I felt my tears free falling as my husband rushed over wrapping his arms around me and our son. I held onto him for dear life, afraid to let go.

"Are you two okay?" Damon asked, stepping back to look at me.

"Yes," I answered through tears. He kissed my lips then kissed the top of Josiah's head.

"Look at him," Damon exclaimed, shedding his own tears. "Baby that's our son."

"Yes," I said laughing. "Yes." I took a moment to enjoy being with my husband and Josiah before asking Damon to take our son outside.

"I'll be there in a moment," I said.

"Okay," he agreed, hesitantly.

I waited until Venetta and I were alone to redirect my attention towards her. She sat on the floor staring at me with eyes so cold; it looked like she had no soul. I knew for her that revenge was a slow, recurring cycle that passed from generation to generation. Sons suffering for the sins of their fathers. Daughters paying for the sins of their mothers. I shook my head in disgust as I strolled to the front door. I could hear sirens coming in the distance, my notification that HPD was on their way. I turned and took one last look at Venetta, raised the gun I still held in my hand, then pulled the trigger three times. I dropped the weapon then exited the home, stepping out into the warm night air, where my husband and son were waiting.

Epilogue

Damon

When Doctor Aoura told me that my son was alive, I originally thought he was lying, attempting to buy himself some time, but the tears in the man's eyes and terror in his voice gave me a positive affirmation that his words were true. He volunteered to take me to the home where Venetta was living with my son and I accepted without a second thought. I contacted the authorities when the doctor and I were almost at Venetta's home. I knew with the time it took them to dispatch officers, I would have enough time to handle and wrap up anything that I desired. I also knew no matter what was waiting for me at the home the outcome would be the same; someone would die.

When I saw my wife's car parked along the street my only thought or concern was that my greatest fear—losing her—would come true. My feet had just struck the landing of the porch when I heard the gunshot and Octavia's and Venetta's voices. That's when I rushed inside. I would have killed the woman with my bare hands, but I listened to my wife's voice and decided to let fate handle it. I was standing outside cradling my son in my arms when I heard the shots being fired, almost reminiscent to the night I murdered Beau. When Octavia stepped out there was something different about her, a certain level of strength that she displayed that let me know she would do anything she had to for the sake of those we love.

As for the doctor and Kaitlyn, I allowed both of them to live, but my kindness did not come without a price. They were turned over to HPD and in the near future they too would stand trial for their crimes.

I sat behind my desk going over notes from my team meeting when there was a knock on my office door.

"Come in," I said, continuing to review the documents in front of me.

"Did I catch you at a bad time?" Tamara asked, standing in the doorway. She wore a blue fitted, above the knee-length dress that hugged her wide hips and dipped low in the front. I hadn't spoken with her personally since I assigned her account to one of my junior associates and I hadn't seen her since the day the two of us crossed the line.

"No, come in," I said, leaning forward against my desk.

"Your assistant wasn't at her station, so I decided to

come to your door," she said, looking at me. "I hope you don't mind." She walked over then sat down across the desk from me.

"She's on lunch," I advised her. "And don't worry, you're fine." There was uncomfortable tension between the two of as she sat staring at me.

"Well, I just wanted to stop in and say thank you," Tamara finally said. "Cam is a great advisor. Thank you for assigning him my account. However, I would have preferred to work with you."

"You're in good hands," I said. "I taught Cam everything I know about the business."

"Your hands are better," she said suggestively. "But I understand you had to do what you had to do."

"I did," I said. I hadn't wanted to take any chances with things becoming too complicated with Tamara. I felt the best way to avoid that was to put some distance between us until I was sure that she was ready to resume a platonic friendship. I know she said she was fine with just being friends, but women—no matter how hard they appear on the outside—are emotional creatures and some of them have a difficult time seeing situations clearly. Yes, Tamara and I are emotionally connected, but for me that connection is far from romantic love.

"Listen, I just wanted to stop in and chat for a moment," she said. "And say congratulations, I saw the news about your son."

"Thank you," I said appreciatively.

"It's an amazing story," she said.

"That's my world," I laughed; but I was dead serious. I swear there were some things that could only happen to my family.

"So I hear," Tamara laughed. She stood then extended her arms to me. "You know how we do." I rose without hesitation then walked around the desk. The two of us shared a friendly hug.

"You know my offer still stands," she said, pulling back.

"What offer is that?"

"If you need someone, I'm here."

"Thank you," I said. "I appreciate it. But I'm good." Tamara smiled slightly, then kissed me on the cheek.

Octavia

I can't begin to express the joy I feel having my family. It's an unbelievable blessing that at times I feel I don't deserve. After the incident at Venetta's home the authorities went to Tabitha's apartment where they found her dead of a drug overdose. Aurora was responsible for the death and he would have gotten away with it if Damon hadn't seen him with Kaitlyn at the Ambiance. As for Kaitlyn, that little bitch better be glad that I didn't get to her before the police. Period! I had no fear that Heather was involved, but I let her go anyway. In my opinion, birds of a feather flock together which meant she was guilty by association.

I've always said that you never know what you may have to do for those you love or the depth of that love until you're put to the test. Venetta issued the test, and I chose to not only pass, but pass with flying colors; specifically red, the color of her shed blood.

I strolled through the parking lot of Nomad Investment, swaying on my heels with the love of my life on my mind. I planned to surprise my husband for lunch. I was half way to the door when I saw Tamara coming out the building. I smiled then waved as I walked towards her.

"How are you," I asked, stopping in front of her.

"I'm good Octavia. You?"

"Great," I said. "I came to take my boo to lunch." Tamara's expression changed slightly as her eyes took on a distant look.

"What are you up to?"

"I just stopped by to say hello," she said. "To see how Damon was doing."

"You haven't talked?" I asked. I was surprised the two of them weren't keeping better contact, especially living in the same city.

"No," she said. "But everything happens for a reason." There was something strange in her voice that alerted me that there was more she wanted to say, but she chose not to say. "Well, I'd better get going. Take care."

"You do the same," I said, smiling. "Stop by the

restaurant some time for lunch or dinner. My treat."

"I'll be sure to do that," she started to walk away then stopped. "I almost forgot," she said, digging in her purse. "Give these to Damon for me." I opened my hand allowing Tamara to drop the set of platinum cuff links in my palm. "See you around," she said victoriously before strutting off.

G STREET CHRONICLES
~ PRESENTS ~

HAVOC ON A
HOMEWRECKER

A NOVEL

MZ. ROBINSON

AUTHOR OF THE "LOVE, LIES & LUST" SERIES

G STREET *Essence*